Jamal and Me
Freedom Summer

Other books by J. Darnell Johnson

Roots Four Zero

The Opening

Ol' Jim Crow's Jubilee Day Caper

The Supreme Hogon

The Supreme Hogon with comic book ending

Souly Speculative: A collection of six short stories

Jamal and Me
Freedom Summer

J. Darnell Johnson

Copyright © 2022 J. Darnell Johnson

All rights reserved. No part of this publication may be reproduced or transmitted in any form or by any means, electronic or mechanical, including photocopy, recording, or any information storage and retrieval system, without the prior written permission of the copyright owner of this book, except in the case of brief quotations embodied in critical articles and reviews. For permission, email *jamdjohn01@gmail.com*.

Photo credit: Back-cover photos of the civil rights workers murdered in 1964 are from an FBI Missing poster.

The web addresses referenced in this book were live and correct at the time of the book's publication but may be subject to change.

Cover design by Mychal Batson
Editing/interior design by Peggy Henrikson, Heart and Soul Editing

ISBN 9798985940213
Printed in the United States of America

First Edition

Dedication

This book is dedicated to all children. You will one day become adults and be eligible to vote. Even though voting is your constitutional right, obstacles may arise against your voice being heard because of your race.

I want all of you to remember the legacy of Mississippi Freedom Summer and the heroes and sheroes who arose from it. Remember their sacrifice and honor their courage so one day you will not ever have to fight for your right to vote again.

Awareness starts with learning about the history of voter suppression, which excludes certain people and favors others. If you look closely, some suppression still exists today. I hope this book helps you recognize it in all its unjust forms. Remember, voting is your right as an American citizen, so when you become eligible to vote, exercise it!

"We want ours, and we want ours now."

Fannie Lou Hamer, civil rights activist

CONTENTS

Chapter 1: The Winner 1
Chapter 2: Stump Day 6
Chapter 3: Grandma Lynn 16
Chapter 4: Queen Azina 21
Chapter 5: Down to the Delta 25
Chapter 6: 5-0, 5-0! 34
Chapter 7: Freedom School 40
Chapter 8: The Big Day 47
Chapter 9: Canvassing 59
Chapter 10: Three Civil Rights Volunteers 66
Chapter 11: Ma Dear 70
Chapter 12: Registration Worry 77
Chapter 13: Sunflower County Courthouse 81
Chapter 14: Oh, Those Jelly Beans 87
Chapter 15: First-Class Citizen 91
Chapter 16: You Believe Us, Don't You? 98
About the Author 105
Author's Note on Truth vs. Fiction 107
Real-Life Freedom Summer Characters 110
Author's Note on Voter Suppression 113
What Suppression Might Look Like for a Black Child ... 114
Teachers' Resources 117
Glossary of Terms 121
Endnotes 128

- ix -

Chapter 1: The Winner

We had just finished the second to the last day of school. Right off the school bus we sprinted down the alley and straight to our house. Jamal was breathing hard, but today he looked like Superman, his backpack resembling a jet pack. He zoomed right past me for the first time ever. Through the grass, onto the dirt, and over the ant mounds next to the house he ran. He'd always stopped himself at the glass door, but this time his momentum was too great and his hands shattered it.

"Oh no!" I shouted.

Jamal just laughed. "I finally beat you, Jordan! I finally beat you!"

As he was catching his breath, I said, "Look at your hands! They're all bloody!"

"Oh, no . . . Ma Ma's going to kill me," Jamal moaned with a look of dread that told me he knew a whoopin' could be coming.

"It looks like the door is going to kill you first," I said with a wry smile.

Ruff, ruff, ruff! Pharaoh, our German shepherd, barked with gusto, no doubt wanting to come out and play with us.

"Jamal! Jamal, is that you?" Ma Ma shouted out of the window. Wearing her school nursing uniform, Ma Ma ran down the stairs.

The Winner

She took one look at Jamal's hands, grabbed his arm, and pulled him to the side of the house where the hose was hanging. She washed his bloody hands then grabbed him by his ear and pulled him up the front steps and into the house.

"Owwww!" Jamal cried out as Ma Ma poured what looked like a half bottle of rubbing alcohol over his hands into the kitchen sink. Pharaoh stood next to Jamal, half his height, and looked puzzled at what Ma Ma was doing to his buddy.

"Boy, you scared me half to death," Ma Ma said with somewhat contained fury. I don't know how many times I've told you to stop at the tree. Now you've gone and run right through the glass door!"

"But Ma Ma," Jamal said, "I won . . . I won *again!*"

I wondered what he meant, because this was the *first* time he beat me to the house.

"You won *what* again?" Ma Ma asked as she looked for bandages.

"I won the Jelly Bean Guessing Contest again for the eighth time in a row. I won, I won!" Jamal yelled. "But I don't *guess,* I *count,*" he announced for the umpteenth time. "I can't wait to tell Grandma Lynn." He was jumping around with excitement.

Ma Ma shouted, "Settle down now! I gotta put these bandages on your hands!" She put her own hands on each side of his head, covering its cornrows, to calm Jamal down. "Boy, I have trouble counting the number of beats in a minute when I'm takin' a pulse in class, and you can count hundreds of jelly beans," Ma Ma mumbled with a smirk. "Keep it one hundred, Jamal. Keep it one hundred."

"Ma Ma," I said, earnestly jumping in to defend Jamal, "Mr. Thompson, the school principal, said he's never seen anything like Jamal. Claims he's a genius. Jamal can tell you how many pickles are in a jar, the number of popcorn seeds in a bag, or even the number of stars in the sky."

Jamal gave me a doubtful look. "Don't know about the stars, Jordan, but I'd sure try."

Ma Ma wrapped white bandages around Jamal's hands. "Genius? Genius of what? How to shatter glass without shattering your whole body? You're just lucky, Jamal."

My brother plopped down on the couch without flinching. Guess when you're nine you can ignore pain. He dug into his backpack and pulled out his certificate. He proudly read:

Jamal Washington, District 8 winner of the School of the Heart Jelly Bean Guessing Contest, has qualified for the Region Two Jelly Bean Guessing Contest. The winner will receive an Oculus Virtual Reality headset.

He then pulled another paper from his backpack and read: *To enter the contest, you must use the code 3219 on the Region Two website then complete and submit the registration form.*

I commented, "The only thing I worry about is that Region Two is on the other side of town. I don't believe any Black people live over there. In fact, I don't think any Black people have ever made it to the Region Two contest before either."

Ma Ma said, "It doesn't look like you will be entering any contest anytime soon. Your fingers are all wrapped up and you can't use the computer."

Jamal looked at his hands and then at me. "Jordan, can you register for me?"

"Sure. I can do that for you."

"Yay! We can use my second generation Apple iPad!" Jamal pulled from his backpack the new iPad he got for winning the jelly bean contest. He hopped up from the couch and did the griddy dance.

The Winner

"Bling, bling . . . bling, bling!" he shouted with joy. Right on cue, I joined in. We laughed and laughed as we both did the griddy, lookin' just like Justin Jefferson of the Minnesota Vikings.

Ma Ma shook her head and with a little chuckle said, "You two are so lit."

Jamal plugged in his iPad to charge it, looking impatient. "I can't wait for this thing to charge," he finally said. "Ma Ma can we go to the library and use a computer there to enter the Region Two jelly bean guessing contest? . . . But remember; I don't guess, I count."

Ma Ma agreed with only a smile. Pharoah wagged his tail and grabbed his leash in his teeth.

"No, not this time, Fair-O," Jamal told him politely. "Dogs aren't allowed in the library."

When we arrived at the library, all of the computers were occupied, so we decided to browse around a little bit. I looked at some comic books then went to find Jamal. He had several books scattered around him, but was particularly engrossed in one of them.

"Whatcha readin', Jamal?" I inquired. He didn't seem to hear me until I asked twice more, raising my voice each time. This caused the librarian to give me a look that would scare anyone but Jamal, who is generally unflappable.

"It's *The Life of Fannie Lou Hamer*," he finally responded. "And other civil rights leaders from the civil rights days. All of these books are about civil rights heroes. I'm going to check them all out, but I want to read this one first."

"Oh . . . nice," I said. "Hey, I see a computer is open. Let's go get you registered."

I went to the Region Two website, entered the code 3-2-1-9, and created a user name and password. After entering Jamal's information, I clicked on the Submit button. Up popped the message, *You have just been entered into the Region Two Jelly Bean Guessing*

Contest. You will receive a confirmation email. Jamal shouted and we fist bumped. This time, the librarian pointed to the door as she stared at us. Jamal insisted on checking out his new find about civil rights leader Fannie Lou Hamer and the other books about civil rights. Then we ran out under the stern eye of the librarian.

Chapter 2: Stump Day

Finally, it was the last day of school. Everyone was extra hyped to greet Mr. Brimmer just outside our classroom 205. As he had all year, he greeted each of us in our own special way before we walked through the door. We did shoulder shrugs, head fakes, high fives, back-hand slaps, back bends and neck jerks, hair fades and body twists, flossing, and griddy dances. You name it, we did it. Oh, what fun it was. That's one thing I'll miss about going to school—Mr. Brimmer's connection with us every day before the school day began.

When it was my turn, I started off with a shimmy shake, then a paddy cake, followed by a nod, a wink, a shoulder lift, and a head turn, ending with the griddy.

Everyone was lit. In fact, after our greeting, Mr. Brimmer told us, "Now go light up the world!" No homework, no quizzes, no tests, no book reports. No more making excuses for not turning in my homework on time or for being late because I was trying to make sure Jamal got to his class before me.

But in the classroom this last day of school, things were a bit out of control. Kids were playing their music, dancing and rapping and singing along with the music. The girls were off in the corner jumping double Dutch. Some were just being silly. It made me a little uncomfortable, but Mr. Brimmer didn't mind. He looked like he was entering our grades into the computer or something. This was the first time he'd let us get lit like that without pounding his fist on the desk.

Finally, he spoke up with authority. "Quiet, *quiet,* please, and *listen!* Take your seats, students of the fifth grade. I would like to announce the two nominees for student council president for next year's sixth graders—both with sixty votes. I'm *very proud* to say that *both* are from *my* fifth-grade classroom 205. They are—drumroll, please— Kamila Payne and Jordan Washington!"

Of course, that figures. Here's my chance at being somebody and I have to be up against Kam Payne, the sweetheart of the fifth grade. The "all-American girl" type with rosy red cheeks and pigtails. The winner of the class spelling bee. The one who knows the answers to all the questions. The girl who says she's going to live on Mars one day, but only after she invents a new rocket to take her there. Her summer vacations aren't going to Chicago like Jamal and me. Kam and her family go to Europe. And on weekends, they go up north to their cabin and fish and ride in their boat. Boy, my chances are zero.

I suddenly realized my heart was pounding. I gasped for air and looked around. My friends were patting me on my back. I looked over at Kam and she looked over at me. We shook hands, but I knew I'd already lost.

Mr. Brimmer paused, fiddled around with his computer, then projected his screen onto the wall at the front of the class. He went on to announce the endorsements. "Kamila has been endorsed by the main office, the library, and the gym. Jordan Washington has received endorsements from the principal's office and . . ." Once I heard the "principal's office," I didn't even hear my next two endorsements. Everyone stood up with loud applause because that was the

Stump Day

most special endorsement you could get. It could go a long way in getting me elected. Even though it was an even split of endorsements, the principal's office carried the most weight. My hope was rekindled.

Mr. Brimmer clapped his hands and said in his rather halting voice, "Class . . . class. It's time for us to talk about the candidates' stump speeches."

"Did you say stump speech?" Armani asked.

"Yes," Mr. Brimmer replied as he pulled his glasses down to his nose and peered over them at Armani.

"What's a stump speech?" Armani asked.

"Whoever wants to be elected for next year's student council class president has responsibilities. For example, you'll need to be involved in determining the quality of school lunches, what field trips students will go on, how long the recess periods will be, what afterschool activities will be available, and the kinds of books students have to read.

"You have to *campaign* and, most important, you'll want to write a stump speech. In your stump speech, you repeat the same phrases over and over so the ideas stick with the people you're trying to convince to vote for you. If they remember what you say, you could get their vote.

Kamila, Jordan, it's time to write your stump speeches and come up with a slogan. That's a catchy phrase such as Jesse Jackson's "Keep hope alive" or Barack Obama's "Yes we can." The rest of you can either go to the gym or play outside until they're finished." The students ran out of the classroom, and there Kam and I sat, alone with Mr. Brimmer.

I sat at my desk and thought, and I thought and thought some more. I looked over at Kam and she was typing fast and furiously. Mr. Brimmer came over to me and asked if I had any questions. I just told him I didn't know what to write. "I know what to say," I told him. "But I can't seem to write it down."

"Well, speak from your heart," he advised me.

"What do you mean, my heart?"

"Don't write anything down, just rehearse the words in your head as they come to you. You'll know what to say when you feel it.

Hmmm. I thought and I thought, and my stump speech started to come to me. Kam was typing faster than a court sten . . . , steno . . . , you know, a court writer. At long last, I said, "I'm ready."

Mr. Brimmer looked over at Kamila. "I need more time, Mr. Brimmer. Please, I need more time."

Mr. Brimmer paused then told her, "You have another half hour. Once you finish, you can go to the Canva website and create your election posters with your photo, slogan, and VOTE FOR ME or something like that."

Kam and I finished our posters about the same time and rushed to show Mr. Brimmer our work. Kam was a step ahead of me. In the background of her election poster flew the American flag, but in place of the stars were 50 tiny photos of herself. Her campaign slogan was: *"A vote for me is a vote for America!* Elect Kamila Payne for sixth grade student council president."

Mr. Brimmer stared at the poster. Then he rubbed his chin and asked, "Are you *sure* you want to present yourself like this, Kamila? I mean the American flag and all? Don't you think that's a bit much?"

"Oh, yes, Mr. Brimmer! This is just how I need people to see me."

"And how's *that?*"

"An all-American hero!"

Stump Day

Mr. Brimmer didn't argue. He turned to me and asked to see *my* poster. In my picture, I had my arms crossed with a big smile on my face. I also had pictures of a playground, books on a shelf, a window air conditioner, and a picture of a lunchroom counter. At the top of the poster it read: *"When I win, you win—we are ALL winners!* Elect Jordan Washington for sixth grade student council president."

Mr. Brimmer solemnly considered my poster. Then he asked, "Is this what you want to communicate to your fellow students?"

"Yes, yes, it is," I replied a little hesitantly, as Mr. Brimmer didn't seem to like my poster either. But I didn't care. *I* liked it.

"Well okay then. We have two posters. Each of you print twenty copies so they can be posted around the school and at your campaign booths. Now let me see your stump speeches."

Mr. Brimmer took a lot of time reading them and correcting some spelling mistakes. When he finished, he announced, "Now I want you to read them out loud to me."

We both read our speeches, and Mr. Brimmer commented that he thought our speeches were better than our posters. "But what do *I* know? This is for the *students,* not the *teachers,*" he added with a thoughtful smile.

Whew, that's a relief, I thought. Now on to printing our posters in the office and posting them. I put mine up in the cafeteria, gym, and library. Outside, I tacked them on the wall next to the playground and on the large maple tree near the front entrance of the school.

It was time for recess, and I saw Jamal running around chasing a kid. I think they were playing tag. He looked like a black cat with white paws with those bandages on his hands. I grabbed his arm. "Jamal, Jamal. Did you see my election poster?"

"What? You were nominated? No, no, I didn't. Where?"

I pointed to the closest one on the wall. "Over there, Jamal, over there."

We walked over to the wall and he read it. "I like, I like it, Jordan. Who are you running against?" Jamal asked.

Only the all-American girl Kam Payne."

"Kam Payne?" Jamal questioned. "Think you got a shot?'

"Jamal, can't you read? *When I win, you win—we are ALL winners!*"

"Hope you're right. Good luck!" Jamal yelled as he ran off to continue chasing that boy around the playground.

Back in the classroom, the kids kept playing like it was still recess. Mr. Brimmer was back on his computer, seeming to ignore all the laughter, horseplay, and misbehavior.

I moved to the corner of the room so I could rehearse my stump speech. I whispered the words over and over to remember them because I didn't want to read from a script. I thought it would probably get me more votes if my speech looked like it came "from the heart," as Mr. Brimmer said. The more I practiced, the more I rewrote my speech in my head. I was glad the other kids kind of ignored me. I think they knew I was a little nervous so they gave me my space.

When I looked over at Kam, she seemed very mature as she talked quietly with some of her girlfriends on the other side of the room. *I wonder what she thinks about me. Look at her. She doesn't have a care in the world. She probably thinks I'm no match for her. She looks so relaxed and I'm so nervous.*

Somebody put hands on my shoulders. It was Mr. Brimmer. "Son, are you ready? I noticed you over here rehearsing. Do you need any help?"

"No, no I don't," I said as I looked over at Kam, who didn't need anybody's help. "I can't wait until lunch. I'll be ready."

Stump Day

"Don't sweat it, Jordan. Just do your best," Mr. Brimmer said with a smile and a rub on my shoulder. I nodded, but not very convincingly.

It was now time for the fourth-grade lunch block to eat. Seein' as it was the last day of school, we were getting pizza. I love pizza, but my stomach wouldn't let me eat it because I was too nervous. I did drink a Hi-C orange drink. That seemed to settle my stomach. I asked Mr. Brimmer who was going to give their stump speech first. He said he'd flip a coin.

The kids were busy eating when he asked Kam and me to come over. "Jordan, since your name starts with J and Kamila's starts with K, you will choose heads or tails because J comes before K." Mr. Brimmer pulled a shiny quarter out of his pocket. He set the coin on top of his thumb. "What's your call, Jordan?"

"Heads," I said.

Almost before I got the word out, he was flipping the coin. "Heads it is," Mr. Brimmer announced.

I flashed a quick smile. Mr. Brimmer then walked me over to where I'd give my speech. On that side of the room stood the school principal Mr. Thompson, the head librarian Mrs. Swanson, and the audio/visual lady from the auditorium. My people, my endorsements. *Impressive,* I thought. I didn't know the audio/visual lady's name, but she seemed to know me as I walked toward the lectern. "Good luck, Jordan," she said with a proud smile.

Then Mr. Brimmer stopped me and pointed at the stump. Wow! It was the artificial tree stump from Mr. Brimmer's class. The same kinda stump, he'd told us, that President Lincoln had used to make some of his speeches. I stepped up onto the stump and felt ten feet tall.

Mr. Brimmer grabbed a microphone on a stand and put it in front of me. First, he got the attention of the kids and faculty and urged them to be quiet. He announced my name and told everyone how I'd been practicing. He announced the endorsements I had, too. "And without further ado," he said, "here's the first candidate for the sixth-grade student council, Jordan Washington." People applauded lightly. I wished Jamal coulda been there. He'd tell me straight how I did.

I took hold of the microphone and pulled it toward me. As I cleared my throat, the mic squealed. Mr. Brimmer motioned for me to push it back a little from my face.

Then I spoke. "If you elect me as the student council president, my first order of business will be to make sure the library has more diverse and up-to-date books. Our books are old, and we need some more written by Blacks and other people of color. We all need to know our own history.

"The second thing I will do is ask for playground equipment that's not only new but safe for both the very little kids and the older kids. I will also strongly push for what's called an inclusive playground. A playground for kids of all abilities—just like the one I saw in a White neighborhood on TV last night." I looked over at Mr. Brimmer, and he winked and nodded his head.

"Third, I'll ask to extend our recess time from thirty minutes to forty-five minutes. This will get us out of our classrooms and away from our computers longer so we can be fresh for the second half of the day.

"Fourth, I'll promote air conditioning in every classroom. It's hard to learn when you're sweatin' all the time.

"And last, I'll ask for better tastin,' more interesting lunches. Yes, lunches with seasoning and food from different cultures, including my own. I'm sure my Grandma Lynn wouldn't mind providin' recipes. She's always cookin' sweet potato pie or somethin' like that.

Stump Day

"Remember, we're all winners, and we will win . . . we will win . . . we will win . . . we will win . . . we will win!"

I was surprised to hear all the students and faculty clapping loudly. Some were cheering, "Way to go Jordan!" and "Jordan, you're the best!" And the cheers were also coming from the faculty. I stepped down from the stump and felt I had to do something, so I raised both my arms in the air. This made the crowd applaud even louder. *I guess that wasn't too bad after all.* I looked for Mr. Brimmer's reaction, and he smiled and nodded, smiled and nodded.

Mrs. Seward was on the other side of the cafeteria, where Kam was to speak. Suddenly all the attention was no longer on me. Everyone turned to where Kam was waiting. Someone had moved the stump and microphone to her side, and she was already standing on it, ready to speak. She was glowing with confidence as if she knew she was going to win.

I got nervous and began to walk farther and farther away, toward the back of the room. I decided at that moment I didn't want to hear her speech. I told Mr. Brimmer I had to go to the bathroom. When I returned, everyone was clapping and shouting, "Kam Payne, Kam Payne, Kam Payne!" To me, it sounded like they were shouting campaign, campaign, campaign, which I thought was a smart play on words.

Soon the students were filling out their election forms and dropping them into a box marked Ballot Box. The principal, Mr. Thompson, was given the results of the election. He looked at all of the ballots and counted them all. He then grabbed the microphone and talked about what wonderful stump speeches and posters we both had. "But," he said, "there can only be one winner, and the winner with sixty-five votes is Kamilla Payne, room 205!"

My head dropped, but I quickly lifted it and inhaled.

Jamal and Me: Freedom Summer

Mr. Thompson went on to say, "Elections are about your power to influence others and persuade them to vote for you. The voting process is what our country is built on. One person, one vote. Let's give our love and support to our new sixth-grade student council so we all can win."

That was my *slogan,* I thought. I shrugged my shoulders, went and congratulated Kam, and returned to my classroom to finish my last day of school before summer vacation.

Chapter 3: Grandma Lynn

It was Saturday morning and Jamal and me were sitting at the breakfast table eating our cereal. Ma Ma reminded us that Grandma Lynn would be coming soon. "We know, Ma ma, we know," I said. "We never forget when Grandma Lynn is coming."

"Yeah, and I can't wait to tell her about my qualification for the Region Two contest next week," Jamal added with a happy face.

"And I can't wait to tell her I lost the election," I said, making an ugly face.

I looked out the window and then at the clock and then out the window and back at the clock. Jamal placed his bowl in the sink and walked to the bathroom, then I wiped my face and placed my bowl in the sink. Before I knew it, Jamal had opened the front door and was running across the street to meet Grandma Lynn. Of course, I wasn't far behind.

We watched the city bus coming from a block away. When it arrived, Grandma Lynn was the first to get off. We both gave her a big hug, and she asked, "What's new?" as she always did. "Oh no, child! Your hands!" she exclaimed with a look of concern when she saw Jamal's bandages.

Jamal and Me: Freedom Summer

Jamal ignored her worry. "Grandma, Grandma! I won first prize in the school jelly bean guessing contest. But I'm better than all the rest because I don't guess, I count."

I interrupted Jamal and said, "Grandma Lynn, I got bad news before Jamal tells you his good news. I lost the student council election."

"Well, son," Grandma said while giving me a hug, just be glad some people voted for you." She turned to Jamal. "Now what about this jelly bean guessing contest? Son, you *always* win. What makes this time different?" she asked with a smile as she walked into the house with us trailing right behind her.

"Grandma," Jamal said, "I qualified for the Region Two contest next week. Let me show you what I won." Jamal picked up his certificate and showed it to Grandma Lynn.

"Nice, real nice," Grandma Lynn said with her usual warm smile.

"But that's not all," Jamal added as he ran into our bedroom and returned with his new second generation iPad.

"What's that?" asked Grandma Lynn.

"It's an *iPad,* Grandma!" Jamal replied, looking a little surprised she didn't seem to know.

"Boy, you know I don't know anything about those electronic devices. She turned and looked at Ma Ma washing dishes and said, "Sharaya, you know more 'bout that kinda thing than I do." She arched her back and put both hands on her hips. Ma Ma dried her hands and came over to give Grandma a hug.

Ma Ma got ready to go do her shopping and other errands as she always did on Saturday, and we were happy we'd have Grandma all to ourselves.

Soon Ma Ma was at the door with her purse in one hand and bus card in the other. "I'll be back in a few hours. Hope you all have fun."

Grandma Lynn

"Jelly bean guessing—I mean counting—contest champion, huh?" Grandma Lynn pondered out loud.

"No, Grandma," Jamal jumped in to correct her. "Right now, I'm only champion of the third grade at my school—but I'm lookin' to win the *state* championship of jelly bean guessing . . . 'cept I count."

Grandma looked up into the air and then turned to Jamal and said with a chuckle, "Boy, if only you'd have been around when my mother, your great grandmother, was still alive down in the Mississippi Delta. You could've helped your great grandmother vote. Her name was Mary Jo Washington, but all of us kids and grandkids called her Ma Dear."

"How could Jamal have helped someone vote?" I asked. "Let alone Great Grandma Mary Jo . . . I mean Ma Dear?"

Grandma Lynn explained that back in the Delta area of Mississippi where she was born and raised, White people tried to scare African Americans and discourage them from voting. They didn't want Blacks to have any say in how their communities were run. Grandma told us Whites would have Blacks take a so-called literacy test, which they had to pass before they could register to vote. At the courthouse where Ma Dear tried to register, she had to guess how many jelly beans were in a jar. She never got it right, so she was never able to vote. "Voting is our most precious liberty," Grandma Lynn declared.

Jamal's face reflected a bit of anger. He turned toward Grandma Lynn and said, "I wish I could've been there. She would've been able to vote, if only I had been born."

Jamal showed Grandma Lynn the Fannie Lou Hamer book he got from the library the day before and asked, "You mean it was like it is in this book? Was Ma Dear living during this time in Mississippi?"

Grandma Lynn looked at the cover and then opened it up and looked at a few pages. "Yes, yes," she said, "Mrs. Hamer was a friend of your great grandmother's. They fought and marched for civil rights together!"

"Wait a minute, Grandma," I responded. "You mean to tell me our Ma Dear walked alongside of a civil rights leader during the 1960s?"

"Yes, she did, yes, she did," Grandma repeated with her eyes closed. "God bless her soul."

"What about great grandpa, Grandpa . . . ?" I paused, not knowing his name.

"Shack," Grandma answered swiftly. "Well, he didn't want to have anything to do with civil rights or voting or anything like that. He was a man who seemed defeated. He was full of pride . . . and very angry, but he never let it show. He worked hard and didn't start any trouble. But your great grandma was a troublemaker. She only made *good* trouble, though," Grandma Lynn said with a proud smile.

Jamal thought Ma Dear might be in that book with Fannie Lou Hamer, but he didn't see her there. Grandma Lynn told us she wasn't a leader of the movement, so she probably wasn't in any of the history books.

I thought maybe Ma Dear was on film, marching or something. So, Jamal and me went back to the library to look through more of the civil rights books and DVDs. We checked out as many items as we could and brought them all home.

The rest of the day we didn't speak much to Grandma or Ma Ma because we were busy looking for evidence of our great grandmother. We didn't see her name or face anywhere, so we asked Grandma to look with us at the pictures. She found none of Ma Dear.

Chapter 4: Queen Azina

Saturday night Jamal and me were getting ready for bed. We kissed Grandma and Ma Ma goodnight. Jamal said to Grandma with a sad face, "I wish I could be with Ma Dear."

"You'll see her one day in heaven, Jamal," Grandma Lynn, said in a solemn voice. She headed for the couch and Ma Ma headed for her bedroom.

I pulled on my shorts and tee shirt while Jamal put on his pajama top and bottoms that Ma Ma had given him last Christmas. Jamal looked sort of like a circus clown whose clothes are too small, with patches bein' the only thing holding them together. We both brushed our teeth and lay down in our bunk beds—with me, of course, on the top bunk.

I usually go to sleep before Jamal as he likes to stay up and play with one of his action figures, which he did that night. He finally fell asleep, and I was right behind him.

In the morning, I woke up and took a deep breath, stretching my legs out hard. "Jordan, Jordan!" Jamal shouted. "Finally, you woke up!"

"What is it, Jamal?" I asked.

Jamal went on to tell me the most incredible story ever told. He said he met a queen butterfly.

Around 2:30 or 2:45 in the morning, he said he heard a thump, then another thump and another. He woke up and groaned, thinking Pharaoh's tail was hitting the door trying to wake him so he could go outside for his regular bathroom break.

It was dark, but he could see Pharaoh sleeping next to his bed. Because Jamal was stirring, the dog opened his eyes. "Fair-O, go back to sleep," whispered Jamal. Pharaoh got up and walked out of the cracked bedroom door. Jamal hopped out of bed to let Pharaoh out of the house but another thump stopped him in his tracks. This time he knew it was something hitting the window. He thought it must be moths, and he flipped the outside light switch off.

He looked out the window and what he heard became visible. He saw brilliant lights flickering in green and yellow. More and more of the lights kept bumping into the window in rapid fire succession. Jamal looked up at me, but I was sleeping so soundly he didn't want to wake me.

He looked more closely, and it wasn't moths. They looked like little fireflies, flying out of an ant mound next to the house. But with an even more careful look, Jamal could see they were like butterflies with human heads. One butterfly flew up to the window and motioned for Jamal to come outside. Jamal hesitated at first, but somehow, he trusted the butterflies and walked almost zombie-like outside, leaving Pharaoh in the house.

The little creature who signaled for him to come outside flew right up to his face. *Wow! he thought. A tiny butterfly . . . uhh lady.* She was beautiful! Her skin looked like it was spun from brown sugar. She had big brown eyes, arched eyebrows, long eyelashes, two antennae, and sparkly purple wings. Her dark wavy dreadlocks were piled on top of her tiny head. She wore a gold and green dress that looked to Jamal like an African dashiki with its bold design. He said she reminded him of the Disney cartoon character Tinkerbell, except she was Black. I thought this was just Jamal's imagination and his fascination with Tinkerbell. He became more convincing when he told me he felt more and more peaceful every time she blinked.

Then she spoke in a tiny voice. With every word, her arched eyebrows and antennae lifted a bit. "I am Queen Azina, Queen of the Azziza butterfly people." She opened her arms, and Jamal could hear the other butterfly ladies giggle, which made their faces light up with cute little dimples. "We come from the land of Azzizinia. We have heard your wish and want to help you make it come true."

Jamal said, "Wish? What wish?"

"You wished to see your great grandmother, Jamal, and I can make that happen." Azina spoke with happiness and undoubtable certainty.

In disbelief, Jamal replied, "But my great grandmother is dead."

"You see, Jamal, I can make the impossible possible," answered Azina. "The only thing I ask you to do is get your great grandmother Mary Jo registered to vote by counting those jelly beans for her." Queen Azina's tiny face lit up in a beautiful smile.

Jamal exclaimed, "Oh, I would love to do that! But I have to ask Ma Ma for permission."

"No, no, she mustn't know. You can surprise her when you return."

"Oh, okay. Can Jordan come?"

"Yes, yes, he is invited too. You can tell him about it when he wakes up. We will leave at this time tomorrow night."

"But how will we get there?"

Queen Azina

"Don't you worry about that, young man," Queen Azina said as she winked. "Queen Azina has Black girl magic." Jamal gave Queen Azina a puzzled look.

"Black girls rock—you know?" Queen Azina teased with a raised eyebrow and grin.

Jamal walked slowly backward into the house. He just couldn't take his eyes off Queen Azina and the butterfly ladies. He walked right past Pharaoh, climbed into his bunk, and immediately fell back to sleep.

Chapter 5: Down to the Delta

"Now Jamal, that's the most unbelievable story you've ever told. So unbelievable that no one, I mean *no one*, would ever believe it," I said.

"Well, it's true, Jordan. You of all people *have* to believe me," Jamal urged.

"Black girl magic, huh?" I questioned, refusing to believe him. "She wants to come back tomorrow and somehow take us to Mississippi to help Ma Dear vote? What about the fact that Ma Dear has long been dead? Are you *crazy,* bro?"

Suddenly, I became distracted by the smell of Grandma Lynn's Sunday breakfast sizzling in the pan. I sat up in my top bunk, whirled my legs around, and jumped to the floor next to Jamal. I told him he just had a wishful dream, but he insisted it was true.

"Queen Azina will explain about two-thirty tonight when everyone else is sleeping."

I wanted to prove Jamal wrong, so I agreed to go along with his fairytale. "Let's go have some of Grandma Lynn's crisp bacon and waffles," I said, and Jamal showed no resistance to that idea.

That night, I tried to stay awake as long as I could, but my eyes got drowsy. I told Jamal I was going to sleep and he'd better go to sleep, too. I went to sleep, but Jamal stayed awake. Once again,

Down to the Delta

around 2:30 or so in the morning, he heard a thumping on the window. This time Jamal didn't hesitate. He went to the window and Queen Azina motioned for him to come outside. Jamal woke me up and practically dragged me out with him.

Queen Azina told me about herself and her flock of butterfly ladies and their desire to send us back in time to see our great grandmother in Mississippi. I admit she had me believing! I was hanging on her every word. She had some type of hypnotic effect on me—a warm sense of comfort and joy. Jamal was gazing at her with a smile. So, I thought, *What's the worst that could happen, other than waking up to find out it was only a dream?*

I want Fair-O to go, too, Jamal first thought silently and then said out loud. Queen Azina agreed, and Pharaoh appeared next to Jamal. I was stunned to see her magic in action and was now a firm believer in her power.

"Remember, Jamal," Queen Azina emphasized, "you must help your great grandmother pass that literacy test and count those jelly beans in the jar so she can exercise her right to vote."

Jamal and me both nodded, but with a trace of fear of the unknown in our eyes.

The winged Queen circled around us so fast that I couldn't even see her. Our night clothes changed to jean overalls. Jamal had on a straw hat with a shiny blue band around it picturing colorful jelly beans. He also had a feather tucked in the blue band. Jamal took it off his head, looked at it, and said, "Cool." Then he quietly whispered, "How many, how many, how many?"

"So . . . how many, Jamal?" I asked.

"Thirty-seven and a half jelly beans, because I ate half of the last bean," he declared. We both laughed.

Then Jamal looked down at his hands, turning them over and over. He no longer had any bandages on his hands, and I didn't notice any cuts, either. "Hold on a sec," he told Azina. She must have known what he was thinking, because his backpack suddenly appeared on his back, causing him to lean a little as it was heavy with books.

"Are you ready to go on your freedom ride?" Queen Azina asked whimsically.

"Queen, I just have one question. Why me?" Jamal asked.

"Because, number one," Queen Azina replied, "you're young, so no one will suspect you are helping your great grandmother. Two, you are gifted. You have been given much and are responsible to use it for good. Three, you are Black, and you are a credit to your race. And, finally, four—Ma Dear is part of your family, and family is everything. But you have to promise me one thing. You cannot let anyone know you are from the future. Alright?"

We both agreed. Suddenly we got very dizzy and could hear quiet singing. Then the words became clear. It was Queen Azina's voice.

You're going down to the Delta,
Mississippi I'm told.
If you run into trouble,
You have to remember
You've got to be bold.
You're going down to Indianola
To help your great grandma to vote
By counting the jelly beans
In the jar you will note.

Down in Sunflower County,
Many bales you will tote.
Be patient and be brave

Down to the Delta

So Ma Dear can vote.

Before we knew it, we were in 1964 Mississippi. How'd I know we were down south? We stood in the middle of a cotton field. I could see only African American men and women with bags hanging from their side, bending over and picking the cotton. But that wasn't the first thing I noticed. The heat and humidity made it hard to breathe.

Pharaoh pulled Jamal as if he knew where he was going. Queen Azina told us to walk to the plantation house, and we did. As we got closer and closer, we saw a big sign that read FREEDOM, with painted handprints all around it like a wreath.

Once we got out of the cotton field, we saw a tall and strong-looking Black man wearing overalls and no shirt, cutting another man's hair. Many Black folks and White folks were milling around a large house-like building. A Black woman stood there almost like a robot, obsessively sweeping the dirt over and over. The man looked and looked at us like he was trying to recognize who we were.

"Whoa, whoa, whoa, boys. Tie that dog up," he ordered. "Tie him up. Colored folk don't take too kindly to German shepherd dogs here in the Delta. They aren't friendly to us, and we ain't friendly to them. Dogs like that are trained to attack Negroes. I think you know what I mean. You're not too little to watch television are ya?"

"Don't worry, he's friendly. 'Cept if you aren't friendly to him," Jamal said smiling. He proceeded, however, to tie Pharoah to a nearby tree.

Another man held two books much like Grandma Lynn's pastor did back home. The thick one he clamped under his left armpit, and the thin one he had in his right hand. He stumbled across the porch as if he didn't know where he was. "F-f-four score and s-s-seven years ago, our f-f-fathers—"

The other man put his arm in front of the fellow to stop him. "Shhh, Moc, hold on a minute. . . . You two freedom riders?" the man asked us.

I looked at Jamal, and Jamal said, "Well, we were told we were going on a freedom ride, so we must be freedom riders. Did you know we were coming? You mean there are other freedom riders?"

"Yes . . . yeah," I interrupted before Jamal got in too deep. "We're freedom riders."

"You know that's grown folk's work. You two Freedom Summer volunteers from up north, too?" the man asked.

"Jamal looked at me this time, and I replied with a little more bass in my voice, "Yes, sir. We are, we are."

"I could tell," the man said nodding his head. "I knew you boys were. You talk so proper and all. Didn't they tell you at orientation that Colored Mississippians didn't care much for German shepherd dogs? Where're your parents?"

"You see, Queen Azina—" I looked over my shoulder and her majesty was nowhere to be found. "She ghosted us," I said underneath my breath to Jamal.

"Queen Azina?" the man questioned. "Don't you know Queen Azina is make-believe, just like Brer Rabbit and Uncle Remus? Never mind. What about the dog? I know he ain't no freedom rider."

"Yeah, he is," Jamal said in a matter-of-fact tone.

"Hmmm, okay, whatever. You see that lady over there opening those boxes?" he asked, pointing. "Well, she's my wife, and she can tell you where to go."

Down to the Delta

We walked over to the round-shaped woman opening boxes. She didn't even look up when we told her that her husband directed us to see her. Her mind seemed to be on other things. "Are you two freedom riders? Are you Freedom School volunteers?" she asked, finally checking us out.

We both said, "Yeah."

"Where're your parents?" she asked. Seems we couldn't get away from that question.

Jamal and me looked at each other and I said, "Mary Jo Washington is our grandmother." If I'd have said great grandmother, it would've raised eyebrows.

"Mary Jo Washington?" she questioned. "Chile, you have a White mother? That sounds like a White woman's name."

"No, no. She's African American."

"African American? You mean Colored?" The woman said with a twisted mouth.

"Yeah, Colored, like us. Do you know her?"

"No, I don't know any woman named Mary Jo around here. Help me bring these books inside the school house." Jamal and me grabbed as many books as we could, clambered up three rickety old wooden stairs, and brought them into the school house. "Hurry boys; the assembly is about to begin. Find your seats."

By now I was super thirsty. I asked the woman if there was a pop machine in the building.

"What's a pop machine?" she asked at first, but then she got the idea and pointed to a cooler next to the nearby wall. "There. You'll find soda water in there," she politely said. Jamal and me walked over to get some. I grabbed a purple can and he chose an orange one, and we took them with us into what looked like a small auditorium.

We found two seats near the middle of the crowd of African Americans and White adults and children. The other seats filled up quickly. A large circular sign read RULEVILLE FREEDOM SCHOOL. Underneath the words, a drawing showed one Black hand and one White hand shaking. The woman who told us to find our seats walked with a limp up to the front of the room and began to speak.

"My name is Fannie Lou Hamer," she began. Jamal looked at me and I thought his eyes were gonna pop right out. "I am from right here in Ruleville, Mississippi," continued Fannie Lou. She went on to say how on August 31st, 1962, eighteen Colored folks tried to register to vote by taking a literacy test. She was one of them. On the way back home on the bus, the bus driver was charged with driving a wrong-colored bus. When Fannie Lou returned home, the plantation owner was mad because she tried to register to vote. He said if she didn't withdraw her registration, she would have to leave because people weren't ready for that in Mississippi.

She talked about how the next month sixteen bullets were fired into her home on the same night two girls were shot in Ruleville. She explained how she attended a voter registration workshop in 1963. On the way back to Ruleville, some people got off to use the restroom and get something to eat, and the highway patrol and chief of police ordered them out. The patrolman then told another patrolman to get Fannie Lou. The patrolman told her she was under arrest and kicked her. They took her to jail, and she could hear kicks and screams and somebody yellin', "Can you say *'sir,'* nigger?"

Then they turned their attention to her and put her in a cell with two other Negro prisoners. Under orders from the state highway patrolman, the two prisoners beat her on the head with the patrolman's blackjack weapon. Then they pulled her dress up. She said she covered her left side because she had polio when she was six years

Down to the Delta

old and was disfigured. (I guessed that's why she walked with a limp.) Then a White man beat her, too.

She said this all happened around the time Medgar Evers was killed. Jamal whispered to me he read that Medgar was a civil rights activist. Fannie Lou began to pray she wouldn't be the next Negro killed for trying to register to vote so she could become a first-class citizen. She finished with, "I am just sick and tired of being sick and tired!"

She told us that was why Bob Moses started the Mississippi Freedom Summer Project. He invited volunteers, mostly college students, from all over the country to help in Mississippi. That way, they could bring national attention to this crisis.

Everyone broke into a booming applause. Jamal and me did, too. I thought, *What a powerful but scary story.* Fannie Lou's spirit was fearless. I think my heart cried for the first time.

She then began to sing one of her favorite songs and a local favorite, "This Little Light of Mine." Everyone else stood and joined in.

>*This little light of mine*
>*I'm gonna let it shine.*
>*Oh, this little light of mine*
>*I'm gonna let it shine.*
>*This little light of mine*
>*I'm gonna let it shine.*
>*Let it shine, all the time, let it shine.*
>
>*All around the neighborhood*
>*I'm gonna let it shine.*
>*All around the neighborhood*
>*I'm gonna let it shine.*

Jamal and Me: Freedom Summer

All around the neighborhood
I'm gonna let it shine.
Let it shine, all the time, let it shine.

Hide it under a bushel? No!
I'm gonna let it shine.
Hide it under a bushel? No!
I'm gonna let it shine.
Hide it under a bushel? No!
I'm gonna let it shine.
Let it shine, all the time, let it shine.

Don't let Satan blow it out!
I'm gonna let it shine.
Don't let Satan blow it out!
I'm gonna let it shine.
Don't let Satan blow it out!
I'm gonna let it shine.
Let it shine, all the time, let it shine.

Chapter 6: 5-0, 5-0!

After her talk, Mrs. Hamer told us to join the others downstairs in the basement to eat. It appeared everyone had a hearty appetite, as the line of volunteers and students was long. "Mmm, mmm, good," declared Jamal. "My favorite—chicken and dumplings." We got our plates and sat down at the same table as the Hamers.

Across from us were Mr. and Mrs. Hamer and the funny old man who was with Mr. Hamer. We had heard Mr. Hamer call him Moc, and Mrs. Hamer called her husband Pap.

Everyone ate slowly, but Jamal and me inhaled the food. Mrs. Hamer seemed more interested in asking us a lot of questions than eating.

"What're your names?"

"I'm Jordan and this is my brother Jamal." Jamal looked right at her with a wide smile.

"How old are you two boys?"

"I'm eleven and my brother is nine," I replied.

"Where are you from and where are you staying?"

"We're from Minneapolis. We have no place to stay," I said.

Mrs. Hamer looked at Pap. Then she asked us if we were orphans. I told her we were, even though I wasn't sure what an

Jamal and Me: Freedom Summer

orphan was. She then whispered into Mr. Hamer's ear, and he said out loud, "Whatever you want, Fannie Lou."

Mrs. Hamer turned to us and asked if we would like to stay with them, at least until she could find us a more lasting home.

We both yelled, "Yes!" Then Jamal added, "But we still need to find our grandmother, Mary Jo Washington."

"Chile, I tol' you I don't know any Colored person who goes by that name, and I know just about every Colored person in this town. Finish your meal, and we'll take you to our home. Pap has to stay here to finish some work at the school. I'll see if Mr. Moses, the project director, can carry us."

Carry us? He must be a very strong man.

"I suppose you two will need a change of clothes, too. Maybe Mr. Moses can bring you some. I'll ask," Mrs. Hamer said. As we got up to leave, Moc grabbed his books and said in a quiet voice, "W-w-we the people of the United S-s-states, in order to f-f-form a more p-p-perfect Union—"

Mr. Hamer only turned and looked at Moc, and he stopped abruptly.

Mr. Moses pulled up in an old green and white car, the likes of which I'd never seen. Jamal and me and Pharaoh piled into the back seat. Mrs. Hamer sat with Mr. Moses, who had a box of clothes for us.

Mr. Moses turned and looked at us with his big ol' smart-guy glasses. "The dog stays," he proclaimed loudly with no southern accent. Jamal held Pharaoh tight. "The dog stays," Mr. Moses repeated. Jamal reluctantly walked Pharoah back to the building, tied him up, gave him a hug, and ran back to the car.

Just like Mrs. Hamer had done, Mr. Moses asked us a lot of questions, and we gave him the same responses.

Jamal asked, "Mr. Moses, do you know Mary Jo Washington?"

5-0, 5-0!

He thought and scratched his chin, "No, no . . . I can't say that I do. Is she Colored? Is she your mother?"

"No, just a relative," I said with a frown. *Had Grandma Lynn lied to us about her being friends with Mrs. Hamer and marching for civil rights just to make us feel proud?*

Jamal and me looked out of the window and enjoyed the wide-open countryside. "Have you ever been to a plantation?" Mr. Moses asked over his shoulder. Jamal and me both shook our heads no—but to myself, I figured the cotton fields we landed in were part of one.

Mrs. Hamer began to hum what kind of sounded like a church hymn. We began to feel more comfortable especially since Mrs. Hamer was very nice. I started to fall asleep, but Jamal was wide awake, and he rolled down his window. Immediately, his straw hat flew right out.

"Stop the car, stop the car! My hat flew out the window!" Jamal shouted.

Mr. Hamer stopped abruptly and put the car into reverse. Then, seemingly out of nowhere, red flashing lights came barreling toward us as if they were going to crash right into our car. I thought I was dreaming, but the car suddenly slowed down. "Oh shoot!" said Mr. Moses. "Not again."

Jamal looked up and shouted, "5-0, 5-0!"

"Hush, boy. Don't say another word," Mr. Moses scolded. "Everyone, put your hands out in front where they can see them."

The policeman parked his car right behind Mr. Moses' car. I noticed a German shepherd like Pharoah in his backseat, barking and whining. I thought he looked like he wanted to escape and be free to attack us. Now I knew why these Black folks didn't like German shepherds.

The officer strode over to the driver's side and addressed Mr. Moses. "Boy, you're the one runnin' that Freedom School down the road back there, ain't ya? Why don't you go back to New York, you communist Yank! You know the Klan is lookin' for you." Mr. Moses gave the officer a defiant look, whereupon the officer opened the door, grabbed him by the arm, and dragged him behind his car.

I heard Mr. Moses grunt and groan but couldn't see what the officer was doing to him. Mr. Moses didn't seem to be fighting back. Without thinking, I shouted, "I wish I had my video camera! This would go viral!"

Mrs. Hamer looked surprised. "What? A virus? And you own a video camera?"

"No, I only *wish* I had one," I said nervously.

"Oh. Even if you had one, it wouldn't do no good. We get beaten on television all the time and nothin' ever changes," Mrs. Hamer replied.

In a matter of minutes, the police officer shoved Mr. Moses back to the car. Mr. Moses stumbled forward a few steps. His clothes were torn, his mouth was bloodied, and his face was red and purple. Mrs. Hamer gasped and almost screamed, but she appeared to be trying hard not to show she was upset. As a parting gesture, the patrolman picked up Jamal's straw hat and threw it to the side of the road. Jamal was furious, but I held him tight.

Mrs. Hamer sat there with her hands on the dashboard, almost motionless, until the policeman left. Then she got out of the car and helped Mr. Moses into the passenger seat, where he slumped, holding his head.

Jamal waited for the cop to leave. Then he ran across the road, picked up his hat, brushed it off, and put it back on his head.

5-0, 5-0!

Mrs. Hamer got into the driver's seat and drove the rest of the way to her home as if she were used to this kind of thing.

We drove past some chickens, a couple of cows, and a donkey before we got to the front porch of the Hamers' home. Fannie Lou asked Jamal and me to help get Mr. Moses into the house. Two girls immediately came with cold towels and bandages. One of the girls seemed about my age, and the other couldn't have been older than twenty. Mrs. Hamer was on the telephone right away talking to someone. It sounded like she was reporting it to the police, which seemed odd. But when she hung up the phone, she said it was the NAACP. They took her report and were going to look into it. Grandma Lynn had told me and Jamal about the NAACP. It meant the National Association for the Advancement of Colored People. I could tell we'd come a long way since the 1960s in Mississippi, but I knew we could still use lots of help.

From the back of the house, a White man and White lady came out and asked if they could help. "No, No," Mrs. Hamer said. "But thank you."

Mr. Moses rested awhile then said he had to go. He said he had work to do. Jamal and me sat quietly to see what was going to happen next. One of the girls asked their mother who we were.

"They're freedom riders and freedom fighters, they say—volunteers from the north. They'll be staying with us for a while. Best get them some clean bedsheets for the divan."

The girl stared at us and looked us up and down. "Ya'll sure are po to be freedom fighters."

"Po?" Jamal asked. "We got more money than you."

"No, silly. Po means skinny."

I couldn't help but laugh out loud.

"Where'd you get that funny lookin' hat?" one of the girls asked.

Jamal tipped his hat and bowed.

The youngest girl giggled, pointing at Jamal's head. "What d'ya call that hairstyle? You look like a girl."

Mrs. Hamer cleared her throat and said, "These are our two daughters, Vergie and Dorothy Jean. And this is Mr. Johnson and Ms. Wallace, she added, nodding toward the white man and woman. They both gave Mrs. Hamer a "don't call me that" look. "I mean, John and Theresa. Y'all both know I ain't used to callin' White folks by their first name. They're Freedom Summer volunteers from Ohio," she explained for our benefit. Then she completed introductions with, "These boys are Jamal and Jordan." We just sat there trying to figure out this new world we were in.

"Why did that policeman beat up Mr. Moses?" Jamal asked Mrs. Hamer.

"They were just tryin' to scare us outta makin' somethin' of ourselves at the Freedom School," she explained. "Ya see, in the South, if Colored folk ever want to be somebody—like get an education, or vote, or have some dignity or somethin'—White folk are always tryin' to send us backward. . . . *But* . . ." she added, placing her hands firmly on her hips, "we will *not* be moved."

Chapter 7: Freedom School

The next morning, Jamal and me were excited to go to Freedom School. Vergie waved her finger in my face and said, "No, no, no. We got chores to do. We're sharecroppers on Mr. Marlowe's plantation. He won't even let us see the light of day unless we do our chores. He hates that we go to Freedom School anyway. We have to work to earn our keep."

So, we kids and the two volunteer guests milked the cows, fed the chickens, brought eggs from the hen house, shelled peas, and pulled water from the well to give to the mule. We hauled some cured meat from the smokehouse, cleaned the outhouse, and finally got to eat breakfast. Boy, we did more work in one hour than Jamal and me ever did in our lives!

"Do you have a can of pop . . . I mean soda water?" I asked Vergie. "The purple kind?" I figured I had earned my keep. She brought me a can from the refrigerator.

Mr. and Mrs. Hamer drove us back to Freedom School. Vergie got us registered for classes in history, English, civics, citizenship, literature, foreign languages including Swahili, math, and science. Boy, were we going to be smart! Both Jamal and me chose Art for our elective course.

Jamal and Me: Freedom Summer

I couldn't believe Mr. Moses was standing there appearing to be unaffected by that police beating except for his obvious bruises. I was also surprised that the others didn't say anything about his badly beaten face. He updated the freedom volunteers and students on what had taken place the day before on our way to the Hamer home. He then dismissed everyone to go to their classes.

Classes were being held both inside and outside. Some were on the steps, others were in the front yard, in the backyard, underneath a tree, and in the basement. Wherever there was space, there was a class. Some classes included both adults and kids. Wow! I hadn't seen anything like that before.

Most classes were taught by White people. In history class, we learned about great ancient African civilizations such as Kemet, which was ancient Egypt, and Nubia. We learned about the Mali and Songhai empires and the great City of Timbuktu. Then they taught us about American freedom pioneers such as Harriet Tubman, Booker T. Washington, and Frederick Douglass.

In English class, we learned memory tricks such as "i before e except after c" and subject and verb agreement. We read the dictionary and tried to learn every word in the book, what it meant, and how to spell it. Well, a lot of them, anyway. We also learned the correct pronunciation of words. Jamal even learned how to say Pharaoh instead of Fair-O—at least some of the time.

In civics class we studied the three branches of government in the United States. We also practiced reciting the Declaration of Independence, the Gettysburg Address, and the Preamble to the Constitution. Plus, we learned the history of our national anthem "The Star-Spangled Banner" and the song "God Bless America."

Jamal opened up his backpack and showed the teacher his book *One Vote, Two Votes, I Vote, You Vote.* He read a passage for the class:

"Voting gives each of us our very own voice. It allows a large group to make ONE single choice. HOW DO YOU VOTE? With a proudly raised hand, marks on a paper, thumbs up or thumbs down . . . understand?"[1]

We could hear oohs and aahs from the people. First the adult students whispered, "He's got that magic." Then the other students joined in, quietly chanting "Magic, magic," pointing at Jamal.

"Magic? I'm not magic," Jamal said with a shrug of his shoulders.

The teacher then spoke to Jamal quietly, but I could hear because I was sitting next to him. "Jamal, most Colored people at this school are illiterate, which means they can hardly read or write. It seems you got a talent that most people don't have down here in the Delta.

"By the way," the teacher continued in a normal voice, "I thought I'd read all the Dr. Seuss books, and I've never heard of that one. Where did you get that book, Jamal?"

"The library back home," Jamal said proudly. The other students murmured and shook their heads with a newfound understanding. "But," added Jamal, "this book wasn't written by Dr. Seuss, even though it sounds like him. Bonnie Worth wrote it in his style. That's why you haven't heard of it." He and the teacher talked a few minutes about this, then it was on to other studies.

Jamal and me enjoyed the heck out of basic math and science, because we did experiments with magnifying glasses, soda water, baking soda, and all kinds of other stuff.

Then, in citizenship class, we learned about the most important topic for that time and those people—voter suppression. The teacher explained all the ways voting was being suppressed throughout the South and in Mississippi, in particular. Of course, none of the suppressors admitted that's what was going on. It was secret suppression. Some of the White people were using scare tactics. Plus, they were always changing requirements for voting to keep Negroes, as they were called back then, powerless. They'd move or close polling places, or they'd say you could only vote if your grandfather had voted. "Now, how many Negroes do you know who could vote back then?" the teacher asked. "Heck, it was against the law for them to vote!"

The teacher said voting registrars would question Negroes at the polling places about Mississippi and American political history. If they didn't know the answers, they couldn't vote. "This is why Moc keeps spouting his history lessons," the teacher explained. "He's trying to get ready to register to vote and become a first-class citizen."

My head was spinning from all the ways Black people were being held back from voting. I didn't even know what they all meant, but it sure didn't seem fair or just.

Number one on the list of unfair tactics was poll taxes. For every year a person was eligible to vote, a poll tax payment was due. So, if ten years went by and you didn't vote, you had ten years of payments to make before you were *allowed* to vote. Now how many Black people had that kind of money? Mr. Moses informed us that the Mississippi Freedom Summer Project had raised money to pay people's poll taxes. Plus, if they were sent to jail for some unjust reason, the Project had the money to bail them out.

Number two on the list was the literacy test. You had to know your civics. If you went to register, they might ask you to recite the Constitution's preamble. Or, say how many county judges are in Mississippi. Worse, they would ask you to *name* them all, which of course is too hard for *anyone* to remember.

Freedom School

"I find it interesting," the teacher said, "that Whites try to keep you from learning to read and understanding what you read. But to exercise your right to vote, you *have to be able to read* and understand what you read."

The teacher went on to tell us about the most ridiculous thing they asked the people to do before they could vote. What was it? . . . Guess the number of jelly beans in a jar. "Now how many of us could correctly guess how many jelly beans are in a jar?" the teacher asked.

Jamal raised his hand and almost gleefully said, "I can!"

The teacher looked at Jamal, smiled, and replied, "That's nice, son, but you're not yet old enough to vote."

Then it was time for fun. We played games called red light–green light, freeze tag, and dodgeball. I saw Jamal sneak off with another boy about his age, and he took Pharaoh with them. I heard the boy ask Jamal if he wanted to go chunk some rocks. I knew good and well Jamal didn't know what chunk rocks meant, but *I* knew what it meant. It was harmless, so I didn't say anything.

When they returned, Jamal told me he and his new friend had been chunkin' rocks in the lake and Pharaoh had jumped in after a rock and was dripping wet. Jamal was surprised to find the boy wasn't uncomfortable with Pharaoh. But I realized why most people around there were so frightened of German shepherds.

"Jamal," I said, "don't you remember seeing that angry German shepherd dog in the backseat of that squad car?" Jamal looked a little nervous and nodded his head.

When we returned to the Hamer home, Vergie laughed every time we spoke. Finally, she said to her mother, "Mama, those boys talk so proper, it's cute."

The phone rang and no one answered it. It rang again, and still no one answered it.

I finally said, "Hello! . . . Is someone going to answer the phone? . . . Ma'am, sir?"

"We don't answer this time of evenin' 'cause it ain't nothin' but def threats," Mrs. Hamer explained. Jamal and me looked at each other.

"Are we going to be hurt too?" Jamal asked hesitantly.

"No, no, hon. God is gonna protect all of us. He's protected us this long," Mrs. Hamer responded.

Then the phone rang twice more, and this time Mrs. Hamer said, "Pap, you better answer it."

He did, but all he said was "Okay. Thanks," and he hung up.

"Pap, Pap, who was it?"

"That was Bob Moses. He said the Freedom School was either set on fire or firebombed."

"What difference does it make?" Mrs. Hamer muttered. "It's burned down."

Suddenly, Jamal jumped up. "Oh no—Pharaoh! We left him there!" Jamal ran right past me as if he intended to run all the way back to the school. But before he could leave the front porch, there was Pharaoh, lying at the foot of the steps looking a bit dazed.

I had followed Jamal out to the porch, and we saw a series of tiny yellow and green lights. "Queen Azina!" Jamal whispered, and we couldn't help but smile at each other. We caught a brief glimpse of her and she winked at us. As she smiled, exposing her deep dimples, the winged Queen flew off faster than I could blink.

Jamal went in and told the rest of them, "Never mind. Someone must've brought him to the house."

Mrs. Hamer quickly bowed her head and reached out to Jamal and me on one side and Mr. Hamer and the girls on the other, and

Freedom School

we all held hands. She first said a prayer and then began to sing the civil rights protest song, "Ain't Gonna Let No-body, Turn Me Around." We all joined in with her loudly and proudly.

"Thank God next Sunday is the Big Day!" Mrs. Hamer shouted.

Chapter 8: The Big Day

Today was the fourth Sunday, also known as the Big Day. Jamal was curious as usual. "Mrs. Hamer, what is the Big Day?" he asked.

Mrs. Hamer looked at Jamal with a proud smile and hugged him. "Son, the Big Day is a day of celebration, always on the fourth Sunday of July. It's a religious gathering like they have in Africa. The community comes together to celebrate their first harvest. I learnt that at the Freedom School."

"The community?" Jamal questioned. "That means someone is bound to know our grandmother, and maybe she'll be there!" Jamal said, imagining seeing her for the first time.

Mrs. Hamer continued after giving Jamal a funny look. "It's always celebrated at the Ruleville Baptist Church, and we eat and then eat som'ore. In fact, Pap has already been smokin' his sweet ribs for later today. Pap has a special recipe to make 'em sweet." Mr. Hamer gave Mrs. Hamer a warning look as if she might tell us what the secret recipe was. "We'll eat them later this evening," she added. "During the day, we'll have brunch.

"Ruleville Baptist is where I got baptized, so to speak. Only without water," Mrs. Hamer continued.

"What do you mean, Mrs. Hamer?" I asked.

The Big Day

"Some group used the church for a 'get out and vote' rally and, well, this is the place where I first found out I could even vote. That's what I mean by 'baptized.' I didn't even know Colored people could vote. Once I heard all those wonderful speakers, ministers, and community leaders, I realized if I wanted to have first-class citizenship in this country, I had to exercise my right to vote. I got registered soon after that. But it wasn't easy.

"Mrs. Hamer, what was it like for you to register to vote?" I asked. "Did you have to guess the number of jelly beans in a jar?"

"No chile, no jelly beans. It's a long story, but I'll try to make it short. When I first tried to register at the county courthouse, eighteen of us all went together. When we got there, we felt very uneasy because a lot of White men with guns were there. They told all of us but two to leave the courthouse. I was one of the two who stayed. The clerk gave me the sixteenth section of the Mississippi constitution. He asked me to write it down word for word, with commas and periods and all that stuff. Then he asked me to say what it meant—and I couldn't. Heck, I didn't understand it much at all. Later I found out that even educated peoples didn't do well with it, so I didn't feel so bad."

"Then what happened?" Jamal asked with a face full of curiosity. "How did you get registered?"

"Well, when I returned to my home of eighteen years, Pap had been told by the landowner that he was mad at me for tryin' to register to vote. He said I either had to withdraw my registration or get out. I never told him I didn't pass. I tried not to sound too nasty, but I told him I didn't go down to register for him, I went down to register for myself. This made him even madder, and needless to say, we no longer had a home.

"Later in the fall, I went to register again. This time, due to God's grace and a kindhearted clerk, I passed after tellin' her what a different section of the constitution meant. I really didn't know what I was talkin' about, but I'd become more educated from attendin' those civil rights leadership classes. Maybe that helped me, or it just might've been the grace of God.

"So, this is the first Big Day that I have that freedom kinda feeling."

"Sounds like this should be called Freedom Sunday," Jamal suggested.

"Hmmm," Mrs. Hamer mused. "Freedom Sunday. You might be onto somethin', Jamal."

"I can't wait," Jamal said as he hugged Mrs. Hamer.

"What—to vote?" Mrs. Hamer asked.

"No, to *eat*," Jamal said. Mrs. Hamer hugged him again and laughed.

Mr. Hamer was dressed in his finest suit, and while tying his tie, he said to Jamal and me, "Boys, I have suits for you from the Freedom School. Put these on—and Jamal, you won't be wearin' that hat." Jamal frowned, but he took his suit and went to get dressed.

As I was leaving to put on my suit, Mrs. Hamer smiled at Mr. Hamer and said, "Pap, they're just like the boys you always wanted." He looked at her and grinned.

All six of us hopped into Mr. Hamer's green and white car and headed off to Ruleville Baptist Church. The closer we got to the church, the more and more people we saw walking along the dirt road waving, laughing, and kiddin' around. Mr. Hamer beeped his horn at their many friends along the way. Others honked or waved back.

Black people and White Freedom School teachers and other volunteers walked with signs that said things such as, "We demand voting rights NOW" and "We march for first-class citizenship."

The Big Day

"Wow, Mrs. Hamer!" Jamal exclaimed with big eyes. "I want to march with a sign!"

Mr. Hamer commented, "I never seen this many people at the Big Day before. No one even looks scared. Most people would fear that a church with so many people protestin' would be a target for White folks." He then pointed up at the church steeple. "Looky there, boys. That steeple is a beacon for the people of Ruleville."

Like ants walking into their mound from all directions, the people walked slowly into the church, one giving way to the other. Jamal and me felt special as we walked in our 1964 suits with clip-on black bowties. We all marched through the sanctuary and back outside into the courtyard, where many, many tables and chairs awaited us. The Hamers found their seats, as their table was one of the few that had names on it.

Finally, everyone was seated, or at least those they could get in. The courtyard was full, but more people had to stand around outside. That was better than inside the church, though. It was so hot inside that Jamal and me, for two, were happy to be outside in the courtyard. At least a slight breeze blew from time to time.

Moc was there by himself, handing out programs to people. Every time he handed out a program, he'd say things such as, "Give me your t-t-tired, your p-p-poor, your huddled masses" and "Give me lib-lib-liberty or give me d-d-death." Then he would ask, "P-p-program? . . . P-p-program . . . ?"

Then four men and women entered from the right side of the courtyard, headed toward the front. Wearing red-and-gold-striped robes, they stepped and paused, stepped and paused. As they began to march, three other rows of men and women marched toward the front of the courtyard. Step, pause, step, pause. I heard a hum, and then they all began to sing the same song—"He Never Failed Me Yet."

Jamal and Me: Freedom Summer

They all met at the courtyard altar and finished the song. Reverend Joseph Terry read a scripture from Romans 8:31: "If God is for us, who can be against us." After a few announcements and a prayer, children younger than Jamal and me skipped out to the front of the courtyard while holding hands. They sang and performed a skit about the baby Jesus being born in a manger.

A man from one of the front rows walked up and announced upcoming church activities and recognized some birthdays and anniversaries.

Then, to a loud applause, Mrs. Hamer stood up and bowed. She slowly limped up to the front of the courtyard, grabbed the microphone, and turned that church into her own concert. She started with "Yes, Jesus Loves Me" and ended with her favorite, "This Little Light of Mine." Wow! Mrs. Hamer had people jumping out of their seats and even crying. It didn't take long before everyone was on their feet singing, waving one hand in the air back and forth.

Reverend Terry grabbed the microphone. Laughing, he said to Mrs. Hamer, "Stop, stop! You gonna make me have a heart attack!"

Six ushers, including Moc, went row by row passing an offering plate. I don't know how much money they collected, but it had to be quite a bit. Moc continued to spout political info as the plate came back to him with money in it. I didn't see much small change on those plates—only bills. And I thought everyone around there was poor. Guess they had their priorities.

The service ended with everyone locking arms and singing "We Shall Overcome." Reverend Terry announced to the Freedom Summer volunteers: "This is our faith; this is our armor against those who don't want to see us free. But God is on our side." Then he gave a final prayer.

The Big Day

"Before you leave for lunch," Reverend Terry said, "please be sure to grab a free copy of the Mississippi handbook for political programs. It's printed by the Council of Federated Organizations and gives the history of why most of you volunteers came down here. It explains the Mississippi segregationist and voter suppression laws as well as the Council's commitment to dismantling unjust laws."

Reverend Terry announced the Big Day brunch would be served inside the church, but we could eat either inside the church, in the courtyard, or outside on the church grounds. He praised the wonderful spread, saying, "We local folk want to show you northerners how well we eat here in Mississippi."

He specified they had Mama Flo's succulent honey-butter biscuits, Mrs. Sutton's collard greens, Mr. Wheeler's pork sausage, and Mrs. McDaniel's scrambled eggs with goat cheese. They were offering pancakes and toast with Mrs. Richardson's preserves, Mrs. Olson's famous fried chicken, and fresh-picked figs, apples, watermelon, and cantaloupe from the McDougal plantation.

Jamal rubbed his stomach like he'd never rubbed it before. "Bling, bling, bling, bling! Let's eat!" he exclaimed.

"Let's get the babies something to eat!" said Mrs. Hamer in agreement. Everyone within hearing distance laughed, and they all got up and headed for the servers.

Moc was one of those servers. "Tax-tax-tax-taxation without representation is t-t-tyranny!" he cried out. Then, "Who is the Miss-Miss-Mississippi assistant at-at-attorney general? . . . Burke Marshall!"

Mrs. Hamer's friends kept interrupting our feast. First, Mr. Moses stopped by to talk to us. Then Mrs. Hamer introduced us to everybody who stopped by the table. They would most often ask who we were and Mrs. Hamer would reply, "They're freedom fighters from the north."

They'd usually respond with something like, "This ain't no place for chilren to be" and "You two sure are brave little ones. Bless your hearts."

"They're lookin' for their grandmother," Mrs. Hamer would add.

That was when Jamal would ask, "Do you know Mary Jo Washington?" And with little hesitation they would say no.

Mrs. Hamer had invited a Mrs. Lewis and her nine-year-old son Manny to sit and eat with us. Manny sat next to Jamal, and I sat next to the Hamer girls. Mrs. Hamer asked Mrs. Lewis where Mr. Lewis was. She nodded toward the other side of the room, where he was talking to Reverend Terry. Mrs. Hamer raised an eyebrow and commented, "I know he wants to be the Reverend's associate pastor one day."

Mrs. Hamer asked Mrs. Lewis if she thought she and Mr. Lewis would be able to get away to vote this year.

Mrs. Lewis gave her a defeated look. "Doubt it, Fannie. On election day, we have to stay at our employers' home to work while they go and vote. They know that by the time they get back, the polls will have closed." Mrs. Hamer suggested making up a lie, but Mrs. Lewis shook her head. "I ain't as brave as you, Fannie. We don't wanna lose our jobs."

After that downer, we all talked and laughed, talked and laughed. Jamal and Manny were roughhousing under and around the table. I asked the Hamers if Jamal and me could go outside of the courtyard and play. They agreed and said to watch the big clock on the church steeple and be back to the courtyard by three. I told Jamal to com'on, but he said he wanted to stay and play with his new friend Manny.

The Big Day

    I went outside the courtyard by myself into a sea of people. They were exchanging stories and reminiscing about last year's Big Day. I noticed them introducing their children again because they'd all grown a year older. With all the laughter and teasing, even I had to laugh.

    A short distance away, men and women were marching and chanting with their FREEDOM NOW signs. Others were gathering what they needed for the games, including measuring tape, ropes, string, balls, ribbons, potato sacks—you name it.

    I sat by myself and watched, but I couldn't help but think about Ma Ma and Grandma Lynn back home. I was getting homesick and wanted to go back. I was sure they were worried sick about us. I wished I could send them an email to let them know we were okay and we loved them. But I knew that wasn't going to happen as we were in a different time and a different place where email wasn't even an option.

    As I stared at all the people, I kind of went into a trance and began to daydream. I saw myself walking in the wilderness. Everything was quiet, the sun shone brightly, but it wasn't too hot or cold. I was wearing only pants, no shoes or socks. I opened up my arms as if I wanted to catch the wind. I felt free as a bird. Free to do whatever I wanted.

    Then I heard a loud boom and I took off running. I didn't know why or where, but I was running. Off to the left was a farm-like area with tall grasses, but most of them were weeds. I ran faster and faster. I was almost flying. It seemed to take me hours to get to the grass. Finally, I got there and had to step high each time I took a stride. My mouth was getting dry, but I didn't have time to think about it. A voice was calling on the other side of the grass. "Jordan, Jordan! Come home, come home!" It was Ma Ma calling. I ran faster and faster, but I seemed to not be getting anywhere.

Jamal and Me: Freedom Summer

I finally got out of the grass and into a clearing. I wanted to stop to catch my breath, but something kept telling me to keep running, so I ran and I ran. Suddenly I began to itch. I scratched and scratched, but that didn't stop the itch. I even rolled on the ground over and over and over, but I still didn't get any relief.

When I looked at my arms and upper body, they were full of ticks, mosquitos, leeches, flies, and every creepy bug you could imagine. I stopped and sat down, took in a couple of deep breaths to quiet myself, and went to sleep.

"Young man," a Freedom Summer volunteer said, grabbing my shoulder. "Aren't you supposed to be with Fannie Lou Hamer?"

My eyes popped open wide enough to scare anyone. I asked him what time it was. "A couple minutes after three," he replied.

When I heard "after three," I took off running toward the church and scooted into the side entrance of the courtyard. I was running so fast I almost ran right over Mrs. Hamer. She looked at me with a mixture of impatience and relief. "Son, you almost made me hafta send Pap after ya. But I see you're alright. Let's go have some fun at the Freedom Sunday games," she said with a wink at Jamal, who had coined the term "Freedom Sunday."

"Com'on, Jamal! Let's be a team in the three-legged race!" I said. Jamal looked down and then at his new friend Manny and then at me again. "Oh, go ahead and team up with Manny, then," I told him. "I'm going to do the broad jump."

I sprinted one way and Jamal and Manny the other. I signed in at the table and lined up to jump. On my first jump, I made four feet five inches. My second jump beat that at four feet seven inches, and my third and final jump of four feet eight inches beat the second one. Good—but only enough for second place. I was disappointed, but I wore my red ribbon proudly.

The Big Day

I looked for the Hamers to let them know I won second place but I couldn't locate them, so I looked for them at Jamal and Manny's three-legged race. Lots of people were racing, both adults and kids. I saw the Hamer girls racing together and Manny's parents teaming up. Neither of the pairs won, but it was sure fun watching them fall all over each other.

"Where are Jamal and Manny?" I asked the Hamers and Manny's parents.

"I thought they were with you, Jordan," said Mr. Hamer.

"I'll check to see if they signed up for the race," I told him. I ran over to the table and asked for the sign-up sheet. Neither Jamal's nor Manny's name was on the sheet. "Mr. and Mrs. Hamer," I shouted. "Jamal and Manny aren't signed up!"

Mr. Hamer suggested we take the left side of the games and Manny folks take the right side, and we'd meet back at the center in fifteen minutes. When we returned, we all reported no Jamal and no Manny. Mrs. Hamer had gone back to the church but hadn't seen them there either. "Let's talk to Reverend Terry—no, Bob Moses," Mrs. Hamer proposed.

Mr. Moses was in the middle of a sack race when Mrs. Hamer called at him with fear in her voice. Mr. Moses stopped in his tracks and ran over to us. Mrs. Hamer and Manny's folks told him the boys were missing. "I need to use the church phone," he said.

As Mr. Moses left, Vergie told Mrs. Hamer that someone had seen them leave the church grounds. "They went that way," she said, pointing toward the road leaving the church. Mr. Moses returned and said he contacted the Freedom Summer office and they'd be conducting a patrol of the area near the church.

Mrs. Hamer was shaking her head, angry with herself. "I never should've let that boy out of my sight!" she shrieked. Mr. Hamer hugged her and Manny's folks embraced her, too. The Hamers grabbed and hugged me as well. I said a prayer for Queen Azina to come and rescue Jamal and Manny.

We headed toward the road when we saw Jamal and Manny walking and then running toward us. They had their pant legs rolled up to their thighs and both were holding their shoes. They were sopping wet.

Moc stood off to the side of the road saying, 'Praise God, Praise G-G-God." Then he went on to mutter, "M-M-Mississippi is one of only f-f-five states that elects its state officials in odd num-num-numbered years. Those f-f-four other states bein' Ken-Ken-tucky, L-L-Louisiana, New J-J-Jersey, and Vir-Vir-Virginia."

Mrs. Lewis shouted out to Manny, "Boy, have you lost your mind? You decided to take a swim, huh? You know you worried us half to death. Uhh, oh my! You smell like turpentine!"

"Mama," Manny tried to explain, "What happened was we decided to take a walk because Jamal wanted to see what Mississippi was like. I took him across that field," he said, pointing to the high grass and wooded area.

"Oh, I see," Mrs. Lewis said. "Those chiggers got a hold of ya, didn't they?"

"Yeah," answered Jamal. "And Manny said we had to pour gasoline on ourselves to kill 'em. So, we went to the gasoline station and the man poured gasoline all over us."

"Boys, you did the right thing," Mr. Hamer said. "No other way to get those chiggers off than to pour gasoline all over 'em."

Even though Mrs. Hamer was glad to see them, she was not happy about the clothes. "Chile," she said to Jamal, "you ruined that nice suit from the Freedom School. It'll never be worn again."

Manny added, "But at least we won't be bringin' those chiggers home with us."

The Big Day

    Everyone laughed, and Mr. Hamer announced, "It's time to go home and take a bath outside with the water hose."
    "Yippie!" yelled Jamal and Manny.

Chapter 9: Canvassing

The next morning, Mr. and Mrs. Hamer, Jamal and me drove up to the Freedom School. All that was left was the brick at the front entrance. Smoke still rose from the smoldering ashes. Mr. Moses was there as well as all the volunteers and students. He had already notified the NAACP and FBI. "We will seek justice," Mr. Moses declared. "We may not see it in our lifetime, but it will happen."

Everybody said, "Amen."

Mr. Moses continued. "Our work was not done, and we will continue our education. For now, we will canvass the neighborhoods to register those Negroes who are not registered. We have to convince them to choose faith over fear. These Dixiecrats are going to fight hard to hold on to their power.

"The welcoming committee, also known as the White Citizens Council, meets anyone crossing the Mississippi state line. Sometimes they follow you, pull you over, and beat you if you don't say what they want you to say.

"We won't have any calvary coming to protect us like in the movies. The local police department won't help, and the White churches won't be praying for us. The White business owners won't stand with us. The local elected officials don't want to be

Canvassing

bothered with us. Once you cross the Mason Dixon line into the South, you're on your own. We stand with the Negro people of the Delta, some of the least literate people in this country, to slay Goliath. To help them learn to read, become educated, and vote.

"Remember, the Mississippi Summer Project is a three-fold project. First, we have to get registered as many eligible voters as we can. Second, we have to educate everyone at Freedom School. Third, we have to select delegates for the Mississippi Freedom Democratic Party and shock the heck out of Washington with an integrated delegation. We want to put even more energy into getting our people registered to vote than they do in stopping us from voting. Voting should not be hard or limited. It should be easy and accessible."

Mr. Moses explained to the volunteers. "Most Colored folk are resigned to not challenging the way it is. They fear losing their job and paycheck and dread losing their sharecropping home and car. They live in terror of threats, arrests, bombings, beatings, and shootings. They're afraid of losing their life, family, and friends. We have to convince them that our faith is on our side and our people depend on us to stand up and fight."

The more Mr. Moses spoke, the more we heard the word "FREEDOM!" being shouted. It was a determined bunch.

"We must go house to house, canvassing in the areas where Negroes live," he continued, "and educate them on how and where they can register to vote. We must also strongly encourage them to come to the Freedom School."

A group of about seven men, women, and children—mostly White—took to the dusty red-dirt roads heading deep into the country where houses were sometimes a mile or two apart. Other groups departed, and Mr. Moses was part of our group. Outside of the barbed-wire fences, we passed men carrying hoes, a little girl scrubbing clothes in a washtub, a man chopping wood, and log cabins and wood shacks with aluminum roofs. Then I noticed a man punching the air like he was training for a boxing match. Mr. Moses told us people sometimes get so frustrated at the way things are, they punch at the wind and talk to themselves.

At the first house we visited, a woman slammed the door in our faces. At the next house, someone fired a gun into the air. At the third house, an elderly man and woman came to the door and sat down with us on the porch. The old man said he was one hundred and three years old—too old to vote. His time had passed. Wow, I'd never seen anyone that old before, and he didn't even look a day over ninety. Jamal asked the couple if they knew of a woman named Mary Jo Washington. As usual, the answer was no.

Leaving that house, Mr. Moses said, "Hold up. We need a new strategy." He thought we should let a White man or woman lead the recruitment because the people would respect White folk more than Colored folk. I thought that was odd, seein' as they were Colored themselves. But the others said it was worth a shot. So at the next house, a White volunteer led our group. Lo and behold, the Black men and women were nice and gracious to us all. They opened the door, invited us all in, offered food, and respectfully agreed to register without any hesitation.

As we left, though, I turned to wave goodbye and saw them lock the door, close the curtains, and turn off all the lights. I told Mr. Moses, and it was back to plan A.

Next, we visited a plantation that had a lot of Black sharecroppers living on it. In order to talk to them, we had to first get permission from the White plantation owner. Mr. Moses informed the owner we planned to persuade as many sharecroppers as we could before nightfall to agree to register to vote. He said to go ahead and recruit as many "Negroes" as we'd like. Then he politely

Canvassing

added, "And once they get registered, they'll have to pack their suitcases because they won't be livin' here." Mr. Moses thanked the plantation owner for his time and motioned for us to leave.

At the next house we went to, a lady who was probably Mrs. Hamer's age said she couldn't write. Mr. Moses gave her information about attending our Freedom School. Jamal asked again about our great grandmother, but still the answer was no.

Our luck seemed to increase the more houses we visited. Some people made us ice tea and Kool-Aid to drink while we talked on their porch, and some even let us in their house. I asked if they had any purple soda water, but they didn't.

One woman said voting wouldn't help her and her family. Mr. Moses asked, "If it wouldn't help you, then why are the Whites willing to do anything to keep you from voting?" *Good question,* I thought. But she didn't have an answer.

It was getting late and we were all tired from walking, but Mr. Moses was set on continuing until we got at least one person to agree to register. That meant we'd be walking into the night. We were told to never do that in Ruleville—heck, in all of Mississippi.

We walked past a building that looked like a store. The old sign on the front read "Pap's Juke Joint." *Wow, I didn't know Mr. Hamer owned a business.* I figured that was why he was gone for most of the night but always back by morning. And wouldn't you know, Moc was there, pacing back and forth with his two books.

Our walk continued as the sun began to fall. Mr. Moses was a very determined man, but I didn't think he was serious about keeping us out all night. The next house seemed vacant, but then a child answered the door, wearing only a cloth diaper. I thought she was too old for a diaper—maybe five or six.

"Where are your parents?" Mr. Moses asked. The girl didn't answer. In fact, she didn't even pay attention to us. Mr. Moses pushed the door to swing it all the way open, and there sat a middle-aged man at his dinner table. He seemed distraught.

"Sir," Mr. Moses asked the man, "are you alright?"

The man just stared at the dinner table. Then he lifted his head to look at us and spoke, while chewing on a twig. "My wife is missing. She went to Meridian to march in one of those protests, but she didn't come back this mornin'. She's been gone all day. What am I gonna do? She should've never got involved in fight'n for her rights. All she ever wanted to do was to be able to vote."

"What's her name, sir?" Mr. Moses asked.

"You're Bob Moses, aren't you?"

"Yep, that's me."

"Well, I'll be doggone. The magic man from the north. I wish you could learn me some of that magic. I saw you on TV talkin' about freedom somethin' or other."

"What's your wife's name?" Mr. Moses insisted.

"Her name is Sugar Washington. Most everyone calls her Sug."

"And what's your name?"

"Charles Washington, but people call me Shack."

Mr. Moses asked if he could use the telephone. He said he could reach the NAACP and see if they'd heard anything.

While Mr. Moses was on the phone, Jamal marched toward the man. "What's your wife's *real* name?" he asked.

"Her name's Mary Jo Washington, but everyone calls her Sug. We're Shack and Sug. She's been my wife for over twenty years."

Jamal and me looked at each other wide-eyed. "Grandpa Shack!" Jamal shouted. "Grandpa Shack! It's you!"

"And just who are *you*?" Shack questioned.

"We are—"

Canvassing

"Long lost relatives from Minneapolis," I replied, not sure what Jamal was going to say. "We're freedom riders and freedom fighters. We want to help find your wife."

"Lemonade!" Grandpa Shack blurted out.

When Mr. Moses returned, Jamal shouted, "Guess what! Sug is *Mary Jo* Washington! She's our grandma we've been looking for!"

I nodded vigorously in agreement.

"Is that right?" said Mr. Moses, looking puzzled.

"Did you find out anything?" I asked in earnest.

"No . . . not yet. But they're going to call me back at this phone number as soon as they hear something," he replied with a little nervousness in his voice.

Jamal suddenly reached into his backpack and pulled out his new iPad. "Do you have Wi-Fi?" he asked Grandpa Shack.

Uh oh. I hurriedly tried to put the device back in his backpack, but a man in our group asked what it was. I told him that Jamal had entered a contest and won it.

"Won it?" He grabbed it out of Jamal's hands and said, "What is this thing?"

I told him it was from NASA. Now to be honest, I knew the internet hadn't been invented yet, but I wasn't sure if NASA was around. I hoped he wouldn't ask about it. Jamal took the iPad and put it back in his backpack. "Let's just sit and wait," I said, so that's what we did.

Jamal tried talking to Grandpa Shack, but Grandpa's mind was elsewhere, worrying about Sug. Jamal reached over and just held him, and I did the same.

Then the phone rang. Mr. Moses asked if he could answer. After a short conversation, he hung up the phone and walked over to Grandpa Shack. "She's alive and well."

"Yay!" we boys shouted, and the other canvassers clapped. Mr. Moses told everyone she'd been in jail overnight, but she'd be here in the morning on the Trailways bus.

"Can we stay with Grandpa Shack?" Jamal asked.

Mr. Moses asked Shack if it was okay if we stayed with him until his wife arrived. He nodded yes. "You don't want to be out at night no-way. Shoot, just the thought of bein' in the dark with no streetlights scares me. Every time a car drives by it makes me quake."

I asked who the child was. *Could it be Grandma Lynn? No, it couldn't be.* I asked if the child was a relative of his. I'd learned people in those communities took care of relatives quite often.

"No," he answered. "I'm babysittin' a neighbor's kid. She's kinda slow and needs a lot of attention."

Jamal and me fed the girl then put her in bed. Before we curled up on the long sofa to sleep and while no one was watching, Jamal plugged in his iPad to charge it 'til morning. Guess it was a habit. I couldn't see why as we had no internet.

Dogs barked and barked and police sirens screamed on and off the whole night. We heard Grandpa Shack say, "When you hear that, it means some Negroes were tryin' to exercise their rights as a citizen. Yeah, the White Citizens Council, or as we call it, the 'welcomin' committee,' knows you Freedom Summer folk are here. That's the only time you hear police and their dogs where Negroes live."

We tried to get some sleep but were anxiously waiting for the sun to come up so we could meet Grandma Sug in town.

Chapter 10: Three Civil Rights Volunteers

The sun rose that morning, of course, but it felt different. It just did. We washed up and Mr. Moses said we'd have to walk to town. Grandpa Shack said he had no problem walking into town in the daylight, as he walked into town once a week to get his groceries and other supplies. He dropped the young girl off at her mother's house and off we went.

It took about thirty to forty-five minutes to get there, but finally we did. To Jamal and me this looked like a new world inside the new world we'd landed in. Having spent all of our time in 1964 outside any city, we finally were someplace that resembled one.

On both sides of the street were beauty shops, barbershops, movie theaters, a place called Washateria, grocery stores, and people selling goods out of a wagon. But signs were everywhere stating "Colored only" or "White only." We saw more signs than businesses.

"I'm hungry—let's eat," Jamal said with a growling stomach. Mr. Moses pointed to a breakfast café on the right side. The White people in our group entered the front door, which read "White entrance." We had to go around to the back of the café, where a sign read "Colored entrance."

Jamal and Me: Freedom Summer

Mr. Moses reminded the group to obey all the laws, even if they were unjust. "Once we can vote, that will change," he emphasized. "The bus ought to be here in about thirty minutes, so hurry up and order your food."

"Thank you, Mr. Moses, for buying us breakfast," I said to the Mississippi Summer Project director. He only nodded. We ate and then waited outside on the street near the bus station for Grandma Sug to arrive.

We heard a loud roar and saw a bus coming down the street. On the front of the bus, it read Clarksville. "That's not the bus we're waiting for, is it Mr. Moses?" I asked.

"Yeah, it is," he replied, looking harder at the bus. "It says Clarksville because that's its final destination, but it has to stop in Ruleville first. Let's go meet Mrs. Washington."

We all walked to the bus stop and arrived at the same time the bus did. Jamal jumped in front, and Mr. Moses stuck his arm out in front of him, telling him not to cross the yellow line. The door opened and the passengers began to walk down the steps. Grandpa Shack looked and looked but did not see his wife.

"Where is she, where is she?" Jamal asked. "Could she be on another bus?"

Mr. Moses told us to stay put and went inside the bus station. We sat down on the curb, wondering what could've happened to her. Mr. Moses returned about ten minutes later.

"She missed the bus for whatever reason but should be on the next bus. That doesn't come until 5:30 this evening. We'll just have to wait," a frustrated Mr. Moses reported. "Let's wait over at the Washateria." Grandpa Shack looked dejected and chewed so hard on the twig in his mouth, I thought he was going to eat it.

We all walked over to the Washeteria and sat down. Boy, was it hot, and those washing machines were as loud as it was hot. The

Three Civil Rights Volunteers

radio was on, and then a powerful sounding voice said, "We interrupt this program to give you the following news." Jamal and me looked at each other. *This couldn't be good,* I thought. Grandpa Shack bent over, shut his eyes, and placed his hands on his forehead.

The man on the radio continued. "Three Mississippi civil rights workers have disappeared. Their names are James Chaney, a Negro from Meridian Mississippi, Andrew Goodman, and Mickey Schwerner, White men from New York City. The men had been working with the Mississippi Summer Project, trying to register Mississippians to vote. They were said to be associated with the Congress of Racial Equality and the Council of Federated Organizations. The civil rights activists were all volunteering to help Mississippi Negroes to register to vote during what's called Freedom Summer. Some say their disappearance is a hoax led by the Freedom Schools. We are awaiting comment from Director Bob Moses of the Mississippi Summer Project. The men were last seen in Neshoba County, Mississippi. No further information is available. We will give you more information as we are able to talk to more people."

Bob Moses yelled, "I gotta go!"

Some of the other men and women in the group knew at least one of the three civil rights volunteers. They responded with "Me too!" or "You're not leaving us here!"

Mr. Moses looked at Grandpa Shack, who lifted his head, looking relieved it wasn't his wife. He even cracked a little smile. "Lemonade," he said quietly. Then, "Go ahead. Y'all go ahead. I'll watch the boys."

"You sure?" Mr. Moses questioned.

"Yeah, I'm sure," answered Grandpa Shack. "You're Bob Moses. Ya gotta go to the authorities. Remember, it's Freedom Summer."

Mr. Moses and the others ran to the Trailways bus station, apparently to buy tickets to Neshoba County. Jamal and me and

Grandpa Shack sat there to wait until 5:30, which couldn't come too soon.

Chapter 11: Ma Dear

Grandpa Shack said we had plenty of time to wait so we could go outside. But he warned us not to talk or play with any White people, period. If they were to talk to us, we were to be respectful. If it was an adult, we weren't to look them in the eyes. He told us to keep our head down and just say "yes, sir" or "no, sir"—or "ma'am," as the case may be. "Believe me," he added, "it's for your own good. You boys heard of Emmitt Till, haven't ya?"

"No," we both said, shaking our heads.

"That boy come down here from the north like y'all, less than ten years ago. He never made it back home. Why? Because he didn't know the ways of Mississippi and how to act around White people. So, hear what I tell ya."

Jamal and me looked at each other with frightened eyes then looked back at Grandpa Shack. It felt to me like time stood still.

After that all sunk in, we went outside and stood around a while, but we quickly got bored. We were used to playing our games on Ma Ma's phone or on the iPad. I wanted to listen to my music on my headphones or go to the arcade and play video games. I also liked to wear a friend of mine's virtual reality goggles and play games. I realized I missed being home. Jamal told me he missed Ma Ma and Grandma Lynn. Then I reminded him, "Remember Queen

Azina's message to you. Your mission isn't over yet." Jamal nodded in agreement.

Then Jamal suddenly thought of a way to use his iPad and took it out of his backpack. He turned it on and put it on the camera function. We walked around town taking pictures of things we had never seen before. We recorded the Washeteria sign above the laundromat, the Colored and White drinking fountain and restaurant signs, the red-dirt road, the trees, the Black and White people walking separately.

We got so caught up that before we knew it, it was lunch time. Grandpa Shack walked us over to the place where we could eat lunch. We were hoping for pizza, but in Mississippi at that time, all they had was sandwiches.

We went back to the Washateria and then began to wander around again. This time we wandered into a large field that extended past the laundromat parking lot. Some Black boys were playing catch with a baseball. Jamal and me reached our hands out and one of them threw the ball to Jamal. Jamal threw the ball to me, and I threw it to one of the boys. Soon more boys came, and some had baseball gloves and bats. "Let's play," one of them said. We chose teams, and Jamal and me were on the same team.

Grandpa Shack came out and watched us play. We played and played. We had never played a baseball game for that long. And, boy, did we score a lot of runs—but so did the other team. We won by a score of 20 to 17. Every time Jamal or me scored after touching home plate, we did the griddy dance. We had all the boys doing it after a while. It became a new dance celebration. At least we gave the kids something to enjoy from our time.

Grandpa Shack smiled with joy after the game was over. "Lemonade." He said he used to play baseball for the Negro leagues for a couple of years. He put his arms around us, looked at his silver

Ma Dear

pocket watch with the long chain hanging from it, and shouted, "We're gonna be late! Let's get to the bus station!"

Jamal and me began scratching our legs. I pulled up my pant leg and my leg was red with welts. So was Jamal's. Grandpa Shack chuckled and commented, "That ain't nothin' but chigger bites. A little turpentine or gasoline will take care of 'em."

"Oh no!" Jamal and me shouted and shook our heads. "Not again!" groaned Jamal.

Then he got distracted watching a White boy bounce a ball off the parking lot with very little force, but it went unbelievably high. Over and over, he bounced that ball. Jamal looked at the boy and then looked up into the sky at the ball. Up and down, up and down. Jamal finally went over to him and asked what kind of ball it was. He said it was a Super Ball. Jamal asked if he could try. The boy handed Jamal the ball, but before Jamal could bounce it, Grandpa Shack grabbed his arm. "Boy, don't you have any sense? Com'on, we have a bus to meet."

Jamal gave the ball back to the boy. "Sorry, sir," Grandpa said to the White boy. The boy looked puzzled and so did Jamal and me. Grandpa Shack looked at his silver watch with the chain, and it was 5:30.

We walked at a fast pace over to the Trailways bus station. The bus was right on time. Grandpa Shack nervously paced and looked, paced and looked. Then Ma Dear walked off the bus with her little suitcase. She and Grandpa Shack caught each other's eyes, but before they could hug, Jamal and me ran over to hug her. "Grandma Sugar, it's really *you*!" exclaimed Jamal. I guess he figured she'd *really* wonder if he called her "Ma Dear," as that's what her daughter Grandma Lynn called her.

She smiled and looked at her husband. "Shack, who dis? Who are dese two chilren? They kinda cute. And why'd he call me 'Grandma'?"

Grandpa Shack answered, "They say they're some kinda kinfolk of yours from the north. They been callin' me Grandpa, so . . ."

"Really? I don't know any kinfolk from anywhere up north. Where in the north you from?" she asked us.

"Minneapolis," I said.

"Minnenapolis? Minnesota?' Grandpa Shack said with a surprised look that matched Ma Dear's. "I didn't know there were Colored folk in Minnenapolis."

Grandpa Shack gave Ma Dear a kiss on the cheek and grabbed her bag, and we began the long walk back to their house.

Ma Dear told us she was being harassed and threatened every step of the way and ended up in jail for what they called "unlawful assembly." She said the authorities were tryin' to get her to stop. "But my cause is just and their cause is unjust," she declared. "One day we will have our full freedom with no strings attached. Soon, we'll be able to vote—and then things will change."

Grandpa Shack told her about the Big Day and about the civil rights workers gone missing. Ma Dear gasped because she hadn't heard about it.

As we walked into the large yard of our great grandparents' house, there was Pharaoh on a leash. He was running in circles, so happy to see us. "That your dog?" Grandma asked. Jamal and me grinned at each other. Queen Azina was at it again.

"Yeah," Jamal said. "His name is Fair-O." Jamal went back to how he was used to pronouncing "Pharaoh."

"Chile, dogs like that do the White man's biddin'."

Ma Dear

"Fair-O's a good and faithful dog to us," explained Jamal.

Ma Dear walked into the house, put some leftover food scraps in a small pot, and threw them into the yard. "Just remember, he's *your* dog."

Whatever that meant, I wasn't sure, but Jamal and me smiled at her kindness to Pharaoh. I don't know what the scraps were, but Pharaoh seemed to love them.

"I guess I need to feed these babies," Ma Dear said. She immediately put on her apron and went into the kitchen and took some leftover fried chicken and peas out of the refrigerator. She then began to make some cornbread.

"Boys," Ma Dear asked, "are y'all orphans?"

"Yeah, I guess so," I replied. "But Grandma, do you know a lady named Mrs. Hamer? Fannie Lou Hamer?"

She said she did and that they were good friends. I told her Mrs. Hamer said she didn't know who she was. Ma Dear asked, "What name did ya give her?"

"Mary Jo Washington."

"Chile," she said, "no one knows me by that name down here except maybe the banker or business peoples. When I try to register to vote, I give 'em my real name, but it don't matter because I can never guess the number of jelly beans in that big ol' jar sittin' there. I'm done tryin' to vote, though. I guess it just wasn't meant to be. Oh, I'll continue my fight for civil rights, but those White folks in Meridian harassed me so much. They made it clear they never wanted me to vote. You don't understand these peoples. They have it out for me. I just can't win."

"But Grandma, don't give up the fight!" urged Jamal. "Voting is your voice, and your voice is your power, and power is everything."

"Where'd you learn that, young man?" Ma Dear asked.

"Grandma, I go to Freedom School."

"You know, son," Ma Dear said, "I went to Freedom School, too. And they asked what good is it to have a voice if no one can hear you? What good is it to be able to knock on the door if no one knows you're knockin'? Well, your vote says you're bein' heard."

"And guess what, Grandma?" Jamal said. He got up close to Ma Dear's ear and whispered, "I can count the number of jelly beans in that jar."

I piped up and said, "Yes he can. He's a jelly bean counting wizard!"

"You mean you can guess the number of jelly beans in a jar as big as dis?" Ma Dear spread open her two hands to show how big the jar was.

"Sure, I can. But Grandma, I don't *guess*, I *count*."

"You don't have enough time to count that many jelly beans. Too bad you're too young to vote. When you're old enough, maybe you can register. But for me, chile? Time has passed me by."

Jamal went on and on about how he has won contest after contest in school and how he always counts the right amount every time. He told her he could whisper the number to her if only she'd let him go with her to the place where you get registered.

Grandpa Shack looked over at his wife. "You know, Sug, it's worth a try."

"But I haven't any bus fare, and we have no car."

"No problem," Jamal assured her. "I'll ask Mr. Hamer. He's a very nice man. I bet he will take you."

"What? Pap? I couldn't ask him."

"Just leave it to us, Grandma," I said. "Jamal promised the folks back home that he'd count those jelly beans in the jar for you, so ya gotta let him."

Ma Dear nodded her head up and down slowly and smiled a crooked smile—but then she stopped. "My pocket book is near

Ma Dear

empty. I don't have enough money to pay my poll tax. I only paid once since I been eligible to register."

"But Grandma," I said, "that's what Freedom Summer is all about. They can help you pay your poll tax, too."

I watched as her expression turned to hope.

Chapter 12: Registration Worry

Mr. Hamer came and drove Jamal, me, and Pharaoh back to the Hamer home. On the way there, we saw MISSING posters all up and down the road attached to trees with pictures and descriptions of the three civil rights workers. At the top was CALL THE FBI.

Not too far down the road from the Hamer's place was Williams Chapel Church. As we got closer, we could hear car tires squealing and bottles and windows being broken. Then we saw the church ablaze.

"Oh no—the Reverend!" Mr. Hamer shouted. He pulled into a nearby gas station and called the police. We found out no one was inside the building, thank the Lord, but the church was burned to a crisp. Those vandals were trying to send Black folks the message that this was their town, and they were going to keep it that way. I got to thinking how special Black people must be that the Whites don't want them to read, write, or vote. *What is it about those things that scares them so much?*

When we reached the Hamer home, Mrs. Hamer had lunch waiting for us in the kitchen. "Yum! Peanut butter sandwiches!" Jamal remarked.

Registration Worry

Dorothy and Vergie giggled at us. "Choke, choke! You like choke sandwiches?" Vergie teased. Jamal looked at the girls and then took a large bite of the sandwich, and so did I. The girls just kept giggling.

I informed them an African American man named George Washington Carver invented peanut butter. "He died down south somewhere—Alabama, I think it was." The girls looked astounded.

"Ain't no Negro invented any peanut butter," Vergie declared, and they giggled again at us. I just raised my hand and looked up at the ceiling in frustration.

Mr. Hamer told Mrs. Hamer about the bombing, and once again, she said the Lord's prayer and sang a church hymn or two.

Jamal was trying to find the right time to ask Mr. Hamer about taking Ma Dear to Indianola to register to vote. He was so occupied with Mrs. Hamer, their kids, running his Juke Joint business at night, and working as a sharecropper during the day that no time seemed the right time. And this was not to mention the burning of the church and taking care of Jamal and me.

Several days passed. We walked by a man holding a newspaper who mumbled out loud, "Now ain't that somethin'. First the school is burned down, then the church, and now they found the three civil rights workers' station wagon near a swamp with nobody in it."

I wondered what happened to the civil rights workers. It didn't sound good.

Despite all the bad news, we got up and did the usual chores before going to Freedom School. I wondered how we could have school when the school building had been burned down.

As we drove up to the school, we saw tables outside with banners that read SNCC, SCLC, NAACP, CORE, AND COFO. These were civil rights organizations. All of them aimed to discourage Whites from causing any more terror than they already had and recruit Blacks for membership. These organizations were well known. If Whites attempted to intimidate them, it would get big headlines and be on TV.

All the classrooms were outside—underneath a tree, in an open field, and in the parking lot. Boy, I never knew you could have school anywhere. I always thought it had to be inside of a schoolroom with a roof. But these freedom fighters were tough and spirited. The song "Ain't Gonna Let No-body Turn Me Around" rang truer than ever!

Back at the Hamer home, Mr. Hamer was reading some papers before he got ready to go to work at his business. Jamal suggested maybe this was a good time to ask him to take Ma Dear to register. I walked with him over to the table where Mr. Hamer sat.

"Mr. Hamer," Jamal asked in a pleasant voice, "we don't mean to bother you any more than we already have, but would you do us a favor?"

"What's that, son?"

"Would you be willing to drive Grandma Sugar to Indian—, Indian—"

"Indianola?" Mr. Hamer responded before Jamal could get it out.

"Yeah, Indianola. Would you drive her to Indianola to register?"

"Register to vote?" Mr. Hamer questioned. "She said she wants no more part of that."

"But she's changed her mind, and with my help counting those jelly beans, she's sure to be able to register."

"I don't know. I'm very busy." Then he pondered for a moment and said, "I'll probably be able to take her in two weeks."

"Yes!" Jamal said with a fist pump. "How long does it take to get to Indian—, Indian—"

Registration Worry

"Indianola. Oh, about thirty to forty minutes," replied Mr. Hamer.

"Bling, bling!" Jamal shouted. "You're the best!"

Jamal used the telephone to tell Ma Dear the good news. Jamal was silent for a long time. It seemed like Ma Dear was saying something very important. Jamal handed the phone to me and she kept talking. She was making excuses why she wouldn't be able to go register. Jamal and me both realized she'd been so terrified that she felt defeated. We decided to let some time go by, and when it got close to two weeks, maybe she'd change her mind.

Chapter 13: Sunflower County Courthouse

In close to two weeks, Jamal telephoned Ma Dear and I got close enough to listen in. She was delighted to hear from Jamal. She said she missed us as if we were her own children and wanted to see us again. Jamal let her know we missed her too and wanted to see her as well. He told her that in a couple of days Mr. Hamer would be driving to Indianola to take her to vote.

"What? You want me to go to jail, chile?" She didn't like that news.

"Grandma Sugar, you're not going to jail. You'll be a registered voter. Even if you do go to jail, the Mississippi Summer Project will have the money to bail you out," Jamal assured her.

"Well, make sure Pap brings my poll tax money, too, and I reckon I'll try it," Ma Dear replied with more than a little hesitation.

"Don't worry, Grandma," Jamal said, "we will."

Then Ma Dear had another concern. "Once you guess, I mean count, the number of jelly beans in the jar, how will I know the number to tell the clerk?"

Jamal paused and thought for a minute. Then he said, "I know. I'll slap my thigh. The first set of slaps will be in the hundreds

Sunflower County Courthouse

column. The second set of slaps will be the tens column. The third set of slaps will be in the ones column. So, if it's one hundred and seventy-six, I'll slap my thigh like this." Jamal began to slap his little thigh loudly so she could hear over the phone. Slap . . . slap, slap, slap, slap, slap, slap, slap . . . slap, slap, slap, slap, slap, slap. One hundred and seventy-six.

"Well, I declare. That's easy to remember. You're brilliant, son. I'll tell 'em you're a drummer boy practicin' your lessons. . . . Ya know," she added, "if they catch us, I could go to jail for that. But what the heck. It's worth the risk. I'll be bailed out anyway."

When Jamal got off the phone, he told Mr. Hamer what she'd said and the money he'd have to bring.

Mr. Hamer agreed. Before they left, he managed to get the bail and tax money from Mr. Moses through the Project. He didn't know how much it would cost and just hoped it would be enough if bail was needed.

The day came, and when we arrived at Ma Dear's, Grandpa Shack was outside waiting for us. He gave Jamal and me a stern look. "Y'all keep my wife safe, ya hear? I want her to come back in one piece. Lemonade, ya hear? Make lemonade!"

"Don't worry Grandpa, we got this," I reassured him.

"It took us about an hour to get to Indianola. Every time we saw a patrol car, Ma Dear told Mr. Hamer to take another street or wait and let the policeman pass.

SUNFLOWER COUNTY COURT HOUSE, Keeper of Public Records: REGISTER TO VOTE HERE the sign read. An arrow pointed up to the door. "This must be the place, huh?" I asked.

Ma Dear responded quickly. "Yeah, I know this place too well. And they know me. I hope that mean ol' man isn't workin', because if he is, I'll *never* get registered. . . . *Monster!*" Ma Dear hissed in a loud whisper in case anyone but us was within earshot.

Jamal wore his jelly bean straw hat and a red cape he made at Freedom School with the letter J on it. He also carried a short baton from the school. He couldn't stop twirling it as we walked up the large number of steps to the voter registration office. Oh yeah, and Jamal had a large twig he was chewin' on, just like Grandpa Shack.

"There's that police officer with a German shepherd who's always standin' near the office. The onliest reason they have him there is to intimidate Negroes," Ma Dear said with disgust.

No one was waiting in line, but Ma Dear groaned as she saw the clerk. It was the man she didn't ever want to see again. The "monster" was a large, big-headed, ugly man. He wore wide-rimmed glasses with magnifying lenses, which made his eyes look beady. To make it worse, he was chewing tobacco and spitting into something behind the counter. I could see why Ma Dear called him "Monster."

Mr. Hamer nudged her forward and Ma Dear creeped up to the window. The man was reading a newspaper in between spits. Ma Dear cleared her throat. I don't know if she really needed to clear it or was just trying to get his attention. Jamal began slapping his thigh like he was practicing playing the drums. Ma Dear announced, "My name is Mary Jo Washington. I am here to exercise my right to become a first-class citizen and register to vote."

The man put his paper down and looked at Ma Dear. "Oh you again," he growled as he spat tobacco into a small coffee can. He looked at us then reached down below his desk and put up a sign that read OUT TO LUNCH. "Come back in an hour."

Ma Dear rolled her eyes and looked at Jamal. She turned and we walked over to the waiting area not far from his office. Ma Dear only stared off into the distance, not saying a word.

Sunflower County Courthouse

About five minutes later, a White couple walked in and up to his desk. "Show me your identification," the clerk said. "Then I'll get you started on your paperwork."

Frowning, Ma Dear shook her head and mumbled something.

An hour had passed and we returned to the clerk's desk. Ma Dear repeated the line that she learned from other civil rights workers, "My name is Mary Jo Washington, and I am here to exercise my right to become a first-class citizen and register to vote." This time the clerk didn't look up. Ma Dear repeated her line again and he continued to ignore her.

Mr. Hamer's veins began to stick out of his neck. He banged his fist on the small ledge at the clerk's desk and then looked quickly behind himself in fear that he might be arrested. The police dog barked only once. This time the man looked up. "If you paint your face White you can register," the clerk snarled. "Now take you and your sorry family home." Mr. Hamer put his arm around Ma Dear and we walked back downstairs and sat in his car.

"We need a new plan," Mr. Hamer said. "We'll come back tomorrow. We just have to wear him down."

The next day we walked up to the clerk's office and no one was at the desk. "Good. Maybe that White lady is working," Ma Dear said. But she spoke too soon as the same man from the day before appeared.

"I know, I know who you are. But I'm about to go home sick and no one is available to replace me, so come back tomorrow."

"Don't worry, we will be back," Ma Dear said in a very determined voice. I was proud of her.

The next week we returned to the Sunflower County Clerk's office, and there sat the man who was trying to stop Ma Dear from registering to vote. This time he was smoking a large cigar. The police

Jamal and Me: Freedom Summer

officer and his dog looked on. Once again, Ma Dear said her line—but this time the man asked for her identification. Jamal began slapping his thigh and in between slaps he twirled his baton. Ma Dear showed it to him. Then he told her to complete a form and handed it to her. Ma Dear completed the registration form and returned it to the clerk. The clerk looked at the application and asked, "Where's your receipt?"

"Receipt for what?" Ma Dear asked, looking up at him.

"You said here you paid a year's worth of taxes in nineteen fifty-four. Where's your receipt for that?"

"From ten years ago? No, no, I don't have that receipt—but I'm tellin' you I paid it. I don't know why poor Colored peoples have to pay taxes anyway. I read somewhere that taxation without representation is tyranny."

"Well, you'll have to pay the full amount." The clerk put his hand out. "That will be fifteen dollars."

"Fifteen dollars? We don't have that kinda money. Pap, how much we got?" Mr. Hamer briefly whispered into her ear. "Let's go," Ma Dear demanded. We got back into the car and drove back to Ruleville to the Freedom Summer office to ask for more money. We waited, but Mr. Hamer came out empty handed. He said we'd have to wait about another month before they'd have enough money to pay her taxes and still have enough to bail her out of jail if need be.

Another month passed, and Jamal and me were back at Freedom School. We were eating lunch when Mrs. Hamer came over. She told us Mr. Moses had an update about the missing civil rights workers.

Everyone gathered in the assembly room. Mr. Moses announced, "The bodies of the three civil rights workers Schwerner, Chaney, and Goodman were found buried in

Sunflower County Courthouse

shallow graves near Philadelphia, Mississippi, at the old Jolly farm." We all gasped. Mr. Moses hardly looked up. "I know y'all came here on your own free will because you wanted to fight for the civil rights of Mississippians. I told you from the beginning this wasn't going to be easy—that some may be harassed, beaten, and even killed. Well, if you feel you need to leave, I fully understand. You see, freedom isn't free, and it doesn't happen without sacrifice. It's your choice. You can walk out of here right now—but at the same time, I'm asking you for your sacrifice. I can only say I'll be right there with you." Mr. Moses bowed his head and asked for a moment of silence.

Then Mrs. Hamer limped up to the front of the room and led the singing of "Oh Freedom." Nobody left the room.

Later Jamal, me, and Mrs. Hamer joined Mr. Moses in his office. The small black-and-white television set was on, and there he was, Reverend Dr. Martin Luther King. He expressed his grief over this shocking event and the deep hatred running through so much of our society.

Mr. Moses slumped in his chair and pounded his fist on his desk. We tried to comfort him.

Chapter 14: Oh, Those Jelly Beans

Ma Dear called Mr. Hamer after hearing the news of the three deaths. Even though she was super scared now, she told him she was more determined than ever to register. Mr. Hamer replied, "We're going back to the Sunflower County clerk's office tomorrow."

The next day, we were trudging up those now familiar long steps to the clerk's office. The police officer and dog were in their same spot. This time, a couple of people stood ahead of us in line. Jamal pulled on Ma Dear's dress. "Grandma, is that the White lady you talked about?" Jamal whispered.

Ma Dear looked around the other people and smiled. "Yes, that's her." She whispered a prayer, and before she knew it, she was at the counter. "Ma'am, my name is Mary Jo Washington, and I am here to exercise my right to become a first-class citizen and register to vote." Jamal began to slap his thigh and twirl his baton.

The woman looked at Ma Dear and asked for her identification. Then she noticed Jamal's outfit. "What are you, boy? A drum major or somethin'?"

Jamal answered with his head up, tipping his straw hat and exposing his cornrows. He gave her a proud smile. "Yes, ma'am, I'm a

Oh, Those Jelly Beans

drum major for justice, just like the Reverend Dr. Martin Luther King, Jr. The J on my cape stands for Justice," he said while chewing on his twig.

Ma Dear quickly handed the woman her identification card. The woman rolled her eyes at Jamal and gave Ma Dear the registration application. Ma Dear was so familiar with it, she completed the form in a flash.

Just as she completed the application, a White man tapped her on her shoulder, surprising Ma Dear. The man asked, "Aren't you a sharecropper at the Mason plantation?"

Ma Dear stepped back from the desk and said, "Yes, sir."

The man then said, "Mr. Mason is going to be very unhappy if he knows you're trying to register. Now, why don't you hand me that application and I'll tear it up. Mr. Mason will be none the wiser."

Mr. Hamer looked at the man and then at Ma Dear. She turned and looked at Mr. Hamer and under her breath said, "Shoot, I ain't payin' him no mind." Then she walked back over to the desk. When she returned, the clerk lady told her she'd lost her place in line and would have to start all over again.

Ma Dear again waited patiently, glancing occasionally at the White man staring at her. About fifteen minutes later, Ma Dear returned to the clerk lady with her application. "That'll be fifteen dollars," said the clerk. Mr. Hamer laid the fifteen dollars gently on the desk. The woman took the money, put it in the register, and gave Ma Dear a receipt. The man shook his head and walked away.

The lady then reached underneath the desk and set a jar of jelly beans on the counter. "It's time for your literacy test," she said. She kept her head down, supposedly looking at the registration application, and asked Ma Dear, "Tell me how many jelly beans are in this jar." Jamal started to slap his thigh as if he was practicing drumming.

Jamal and Me: Freedom Summer

Just as soon as she set the jar of jelly beans on the desk Jamal's eyes got wide and almost looked crossed. All those colorful jelly beans were like music to his eyes. They danced and danced, back and forth and up and down. He had a laser focus on that jar. I could barely hear Jamal say, "How many, how many, how many?" Then he began to slap his thigh—this time to communicate the number of jelly beans. Slap, slap . . . slap, slap . . . slap. *That's two hundred and twenty-one,* I said to myself.

Ma Dear looked and looked and then looked back at Jamal. Slap, slap . . . slap, slap . . . slap. She took in a deep breath and stared at the jelly bean jar. The lady was reaching for the hand stamp that said Declined when Ma Dear spoke up. "I would say, two hundred and twenty-one."

The lady's head jerked back. "You are so right!" she exclaimed. "This is unbelievable. No Negro has ever guessed the correct number of jelly beans in this jar. I guess you passed the test."

"Ma'am, what do you mean you guess?" Ma Dear questioned. "I *passed.*"

"I will have to authenticate it with my manager. I will be right back." The lady went into the back room, and we could see her talking to that same terrible man who frightened Ma Dear before.

"Oh no!" Ma Dear groaned. "Now I'll never get to register," she said in a disgusted whisper.

The woman came back and said, "You did good, but you have one more literacy test you have to pass to register."

Ma Dear rolled her eyes and, leaning her head back, said, "What? Another test?"

"Yes," the woman said, and she held up a bar of soap. "You see that? How many bubbles in this bar of soap? How many? How many?" she insisted.

Oh, Those Jelly Beans

"How many bubbles in that bar of soap? Are you kiddin' me? That would be impossible to know," Ma Dear said in frustration.

The woman ripped the wrapping off the white Ivory soap bar. "How many?" the woman asked again.

Jamal called upon his biology, chemistry, physics, math, social studies, and art-science integration skills. When that didn't work, he prayed—and then he guessed. Slap, slap, slap, slap, slap, slap, slap, slap, slap . . . slap, slap, slap, slap, slap, slap, slap, slap . . . slap, slap, slap.

I thought, *That's nine hundred and eighty-three.*

Ma Dear cleared her throat and answered, even quicker this time. "Nine hundred and eighty-three."

The lady gasped again and said, "You are correct, you are correct!" Startled by the woman's excitement, Ma Dear just stared at the woman and watched her jump up and down. "You passed, you passed!" The woman put her hands over her eyes and cried tears of joy. I was surprised myself to see the woman so excited for Ma Dear. Guess she wasn't so bad after all.

"Mrs. Washington, you passed," repeated the clerk. "You are now a registered voter! Aren't you happy?"

"Yeah, I passed, but what about all those Negroes who didn't. Yeah, I might be lucky, but all of us ain't so lucky."

After the clerk gave her a copy of the registration papers marked PASSED, Ma Dear said to us, "Let's go home, y'all." And down the stairs we went. But our happiness was short-lived as we were stopped by a police officer who grabbed Jamal's baton. Jamal hung onto it like a trapeze artist and even did a pull up, but eventually the officer snatched it out of his hands. We rushed to the car and drove off to avoid any more harassment.

Chapter 15: First-Class Citizen

We laughed, joked, sang, and cried all the way to the Freedom School to announce the great news. Ma Dear was so happy she couldn't control herself. She reached into the back seat and patted Jamal on the leg and blew him kisses over and over again. I could see a weight lift from her as she experienced the first step toward freedom. In fact, she looked like a free woman and was beaming with great pride. She said she owed it all to Jamal. "You're the greatest, Jamal!" she boasted. "You're like a grandson to me."

He really is *your great grandson, Ma Dear—he is,* I thought. I kind of wished we could tell her, but who in their right mind would believe *that* story?

Mr. Hamer sang out loud and showed more emotion than we'd ever seen from him. He also repeated the words that Rev. Dr. Martin Luther King had spoken in 1963: "Free at last, free at last. Thank God Almighty, we are free at last!"

We drove right up to the Freedom School. Jamal immediately looked for Mrs. Hamer and brought her back to where we were standing by the car. Mrs. Hamer was thrilled. She hugged Ma Dear, who told her she owed it all to Jamal. "He's the real hero," said Ma Dear. "He was able to count those jelly beans and guess the number of bubbles in a bar of soap in only seconds. He's a genius!"

First-Class Citizen

Mrs. Hamer kissed Jamal on the cheek and affirmed he was indeed a special young man. Mrs. Hamer told Mr. Moses, who asked everyone to gather. Moc paced back and forth, seemingly worried about what Mr. Moses had to say.

When everyone was there, Mr. Moses announced, "I know we had terrible news yesterday, but now I'd like to share some *good* news. We have a new registered voter—Sug Washington! We can thank her for her courage, and we can also thank her little friend Jamal Washington. Jamal is now Sug's honorary grandson. He made what seemed like an impossible task possible. She says she owes it all to Jamal."

The crowd erupted with joy and a roaring applause. Mr. Moses pointed to Jamal and Ma Dear. Jamal took a bow and they clapped even louder. *Wow! My little bro is now an official civil rights hero. I'm so proud of him!*

Then a couple of the children grabbed bongo drums and a tambourine and started dancing around Jamal, shouting, "Harambee, harambee, harambee, harambee," over and over again. I knew from my studies that "Harambee" meant "All pull together" in the Swahili language of Africa.

Moc sat in a chair looking glum while everyone else was shouting "Harambee."

"What's the matter, Moc?" asked Mrs. Hamer.

Moc shook his head back and forth and then looked up at Mrs. Hamer and said, "I-I-I want t-t-to vote."

"You do?" Mrs. Hamer asked. "Are you sure?"

Yes, I-I . . . want t-t-to reg-reg-register just like M-M-Mrs. Wash . . . Washington. I'm sure I can pass that t-t-test. No mat-mat-matter what th-they . . . throw at me."

Jamal and Me: Freedom Summer

Mrs. Hamer bent over and put her arm around Moc and said with a supportive but sorrowful smile, "I'll ask Pap when I get home." Moc gave her a contented smile.

"G-G-Good. But, I will as-as-ask my sis-sister in De-De-Detroit just to be s-s-sure."

The excitement of the Freedom Summer volunteers and students soon settled down, and everyone went back to focusing on their lessons. But the bad news about the three civil rights workers still lingered in the air. Most of the volunteers knew the three workers and were painfully grieving—and I figured some were fearful, thinking they might be next.

The time eventually came to take the three-hour ride in a caravan of cars to Meridian, Mississippi, the city where James Chaney was from, to attend his memorial service. Jamal and me and Mrs. Hamer rode together, with Mrs. Hamer at the wheel. For some reason, Pap didn't attend the funeral. Probably work.

Many of the Freedom Summer volunteers from all over Mississippi were there. I had never seen anything like it. Hundreds of people from various churches marched with signs and pickets, shouting for justice and peace. When we got to the First Union Baptist Church, everyone suddenly became silent, walking quietly and showing the utmost respect. Men took their hats off before entering, and the men let the women in first.

I thought it was strange that Moc wasn't there. He seemed to always be at events involving Freedom Summer in Mississippi. I was hoping to hear him say something about American history. I thought he would be an usher at the funeral, but there were more than enough ushers to hand out obituaries.

Several speakers gave great speeches about the life of James Chaney and civil rights in general, but one speaker stood out above

First-Class Citizen

the rest. Dave Dennis was the president—or director or something like that—of the civil rights organization called COFO, the Council of Federated Organizations. At the end of his moving speech, the man cried. He shouted, "We want freedom now—now! I don't want to go to another memorial. I'm tired of funerals!" He slammed his fist on the podium. "We've got to stand up!"

Everyone exploded into a booming applause. Almost everyone was in tears and huggin' each other for strength. I'd never heard so many Praise Gods, I hear yas, You tell its, Yes suhs, Thass rights, and Hallelujahs. It was truly a spiritual and uplifting church experience.

When we returned back to the Hamer's, Pap was on the telephone. He hung up and said, "I haven't heard from Moc, and no one has seen him in the last twenty-four hours."

Mrs. Hamer asked, "You don't think he went to Indianola to register to vote, do ya?"

"Could be," Mr. Hamer said, "You know Moc. Once he makes up his mind to do somethin', he always follows through with it."

"But I don't understand," Mrs. Hamer said, "I thought you were gonna take him next week. Didn't you tell him that?"

"No, but I was gonna get around to it."

"Oh Pap, you should've told him by now. Who knows what happened to him. You know what they tol' us in Freedom school. Never go to register alone."

Mr. Hamer called Mr. Moses, who told the NAACP and COFO. The NAACP contacted the police about a missing person. Before you knew it, signs with Moc's picture were tacked on almost every tree in Ruleville: HAVE YOU SEEN THIS MAN? LAST SEEN IN RULEVILLE AT THE FREEDOM SCHOOL. His name is Democracy Reynolds.

Oh, so that's what his real name is. I had wondered. Now I knew.

Jamal and Me: Freedom Summer

That night as Jamal and me got ready for bed, I said, "Jamal, you did great—and I'm super proud of you. Ma Dear even got so famous for being a civil rights activist that now she gets to go to *Africa* with Mrs. Hamer and some other activists. . . . But we have to return home. Queen Azina said helping Ma Dear register was your mission, and you've accomplished it."

"Thanks, Jordan—but how do we get back home?" Jamal asked. "Azina only shows up when she wants to show up."

"I'm thinking once Ma Dear and Mrs. Hamer go, we'll call out to Queen Azina to send us home—and I sure hope she answers!"

The day finally arrived when Ma Dear and Mrs. Hamer were going to leave. Mr. Hamer, with Mrs. Hamer in the passenger seat, picked up Ma Dear. Grandpa Shack couldn't bear to see her leave on a plane, so he stayed home. Then Mr. Hamer brought the rest of us to the airport. We saw a group of men and women holding up a sign that said MFDP, which stood for the Mississippi Freedom Democratic Party. I couldn't believe our great grandmother was flying on a plane to New York and then to Africa—and with some very special people! Heck, she couldn't believe it herself!

In New York, she'd be meeting up with world famous actor, singer, and activist Harry Belafonte. He had helped to raise money for the trip. Others going were SNCC chairman, freedom rider, and outspoken advocate for justice John Lewis and other SNCC officers. I had to think hard to remember that SNCC meant Student Nonviolent Coordinating Committee. That's a mouthful! Plus, freedom rider Julian Bond and freedom rider organizer James Forman were going.

I'll never forget that moment when we saw Ma Dear off to New York on her way to Africa. Mr. Hamer said he'd look in on Grampa Shack often while she was gone. I figured he'd really need it.

First-Class Citizen

On our way back to the Hamer home, we noticed all the MISSING posters had been taken down. In their place were WANTED: BOB MOSES posters. They had his picture, but it looked like one they'd take if you went to jail. The signs read: "Negro man, mid-twenties, average height and weight. Wears glasses, sometimes wears overalls. Leader of civil rights activists working in Mississippi. The KKK will pay a reward for information of his whereabouts or proof of his death."

Jamal and me couldn't believe our eyes. Tears began to run down our sad faces. "This place is a madhouse," I moaned. Mr. Hamer said nothing and just stared at the road.

When we got to the Hamer home, the telephone rang. Mr. Hamer picked it up and it was Moc! Mr. Hamer told us Moc was in Detroit visiting his sick sister, who was in the hospital. We were all relieved to hear that, although sorry to hear about his sister. Now we could rest easy.

Jamal looked at me and I at him, and we both asked to be excused. We must have been feeling the same thing—that this would be a good time to leave and go home. We went around to the back of the house and called out for the Queen, and she appeared immediately. Jamal and me had a warm, fuzzy feeling when she smiled. I said, "Queen Azina, we're ready to return home."

"Boys, your job is done here. Your great grandmother is now a registered voter," Queen Azina said with a beautiful and honest presence. "Twizzle, Twazzle, Tiddle Dum, it's time for Pharaoh to come." Then Pharaoh appeared right before our eyes. Jamal and me hugged and hugged Pharaoh. "No more time for long reunions," said Queen Azina. "You two need to go home."

"But what about Ma Dear, Grandpa Shack, and the Hamers?" I asked. "They'll be worried about us—like they were about Moc."

"No, no, young man. They will never even know you entered their lives."

"I sure am going to miss Ma Dear and Grandpa Shack," I said. "I will never ever forget them."

Jamal's head was down. He turned to me, adding in a sorrowful voice, "And Ma Dear's best friend Mrs. Hamer, Mr. Hamer, the Hamer girls, Mr. Moses, Moc, and the Freedom School."

"No one will ever believe us, but we know it's real. They are real, and it's all been real," I said to Jamal with forlorn puppy-dog eyes.

"But remember, Jordan, we'll soon be in our time, and I can't wait to smell Grandma Lynn's cooking and hear Ma Ma's fussing."

"Yeah . . ." I agreed, "but I can't ever forget Ma Dear's beautiful smile after she got registered to vote and Grandpa Shack's 'Lemonade.'" We both laughed with a tinge of sorrow.

Then *poof!* We were back in our bedroom with Queen Azina nowhere to be found. Everything was in the exact same place we'd left it. I was still wearing my shorts and tee shirt, and Jamal was wearing his pajama top and bottoms. His bandages were back on his hands, too. Pharaoh was lying next to the bed. Even the hands on the clock hadn't moved. Jamal and me decided to lie down in our beds and in the morning tell Ma Ma and Grandma Lynn about our journey to Mississippi and Freedom Summer.

Chapter 16: You Believe Us, Don't You?

The sun was barely beginning to rise, and I was still asleep in my bunk. Jamal was up making noises and playing with Pharaoh. "Quiet down, Jamal. I'm trying to sleep. You'll wake up the whole house." Jamal ignored me and kept throwing the ball around the room so Pharaoh could fetch it. "Oh, I see. You *want* to wake up the whole house."

I climbed out of my bunk and put on my robe with no belt. Jamal put on his robe, too, and we traipsed into the living room with Pharoah at our heels.

"Go back to sleep!" Ma Ma shouted from her bedroom.

Grandma Lynn was on the couch and woke up. "What's the matter? You two can't sleep? You can turn on the TV if you want."

"No, we want to tell you something," Jamal said. "Ma Ma, wake up! We want to tell you what happened."

Ma Ma came out, tying her robe belt. "What is it Jamal? What's so important?"

"We saw Ma Dear."

"Saw Ma Dear? You mean in a dream?" Ma Ma asked.

"No, for real. Please sit down and I'll tell you the whole story." Jamal went on to talk about how Queen Azina, the butterfly lady, sent us back to 1964 Mississippi, where we met Fannie Lou and Pap Hamer. How we went to Freedom School during Freedom Summer. He said we asked and asked everybody we met if they knew Mary Jo Washington. Nobody knew who she was, not even Mrs. Hamer. Then I explained how we met Great Grandpa Shack and found out nobody called her Mary Jo—that she was known as Sugar or Sug.

I told them it was like the movie *Mississippi Burning*. "The Freedom School was burned, and churches were burned. Then three civil rights workers were killed and buried. Jamal and me went to the funeral for one of them."

Jamal jumped in to explain the voting victory. "And Grandma Lynn, we went to Indianola, Mississippi, to help Ma Dear register to vote. Those clerks tried like everything to stop her. Finally, I was able to count the number of jelly beans in the jar for Ma Dear in a sneaky way. That wasn't good enough for that county clerk, though. She came back and asked Ma Dear to tell her how many bubbles are in a bar of soap! Now how is anyone supposed to know that? This time, I had to pray and guess."

"But he guessed *right!*" I said. "Again, he was able to tell Ma Dear without the clerk knowing, and she gave the right number and got to register. When we got back to the Freedom School, everyone celebrated Jamal and Ma Dear as civil rights heroes!"

"Can you believe it, Ma Ma? *Me* a civil rights hero?" Jamal asked. He stood with his chin up and chest out, crossed his arms, and looked up. Ma Ma and Grandma Lynn only chuckled. "Keep it one hundred, Jamal. Keep it one hundred," Ma Ma said. Jamal looked cross-eyed at her.

You Believe Us, Don't You?

I came to his rescue with more of the story. "Soon after the funeral of James Chaney in Meridian, Mr. Hamer took us to see Ma Dear and Mrs. Hamer leave on an airplane," I said. "They were invited to go to Africa with a bunch of important civil rights leaders!"

Jamal interrupted to tell them about how loveable Moc was and how he stuttered and kept repeating American history stuff. "He really *really* wanted to pass the literacy test about American politics so he could vote," explained Jamal earnestly.

"Did he pass?" Ma Ma asked.

"He never took the test while we were down there," I replied. "We liked Moc and all the people of Freedom Summer. In a way, we didn't want our trip to end. But we missed you and Grandma Lynn. Once our job was done, we called for Queen Azina, and she sent us home quick as a wink. So here we are."

"Oh yeah," added Jamal, "Queen Azina saved Fair-O from a fire."

"Come here, son." Ma Ma sat Jamal on her lap. "I know you have a vivid imagination, but this story is too much."

"No, Ma Ma, it was *real*." Jamal was wound up. "And once Jordan and the Hamers thought I got lost. Then me and my friend Manny came back to the Big Day games drenched in gasoline because we were trying to get those chiggers off us. Boy, were the Hamers and the Lewises mad. But they got over it quick."

I told Ma Ma and Grandma Lynn that Jamal was the one who named the Big Day Freedom Sunday.

Bein' on a roll, I continued. "Ma Ma, you won't believe it, but almost all the Black families had their fathers living with them. Yes, in 1964 Mississippi!"

Grandma Lynn looked at Ma Ma and said, "Sharaya, either the boys are tellin' the truth, or they know their Black history. What they're sayin' is just how Ma Dear described it was like before I was born." She turned to Jamal and me. "I believe you two. You were really in Ruleville." I smiled at Grandma Lynn and Jamal nodded and nodded.

"Ma Ma," I said, "what Jamal and me are saying is true. I know it sounds like a fairy tale, but it's *true*. I really am keeping it one hundred."

Ma Ma shook her head. But then she said, "Well, it *is* kinda strange that both of you had the same dream."

"Oh!" Jamal shouted and ran back into the bedroom. He returned with his backpack and carefully pulled out his iPad with his bandaged hands. "I took pictures. Wait 'til you see these! Then I know you'll believe us."

Jamal powered up his iPad and went right to the photos. "Wait! Wait a minute," Jamal said as he kept tapping the photos icon.

"Okay, Jamal, show us the pictures of Mississippi from 1964," Grandma Lynn said. I think she really wanted to believe us but was hoping for more proof.

"They're gone!" Jamal exclaimed, looking highly disheartened.

"Gone?" I questioned. "Let me see." I took the iPad and admitted, "Jamal, you're right. The pictures you took are gone."

"Never mind, boys. Now that we're all awake, who wants my famous pan-a-cakes?" We just sat there and said nothing as Grandma Lynn went into the kitchen and started cooking. Soon breakfast was ready, but both of us could hardly eat.

"Jamal," I said, "remember, the Region Two Jelly Bean Guessing Contest is coming up next week."

Jamal picked his head up and slowly smiled. "That's right! Maybe I'll win those Virtual Reality goggles."

Ma Ma looked at Grandma Lynn. "He's back," she said with a grin.

You Believe Us, Don't You?

When showtime came, Jamal was all hyped about winning the jelly bean guessing contest. When the four of us got there, we saw a sign that read CHECK IN HERE. The line was long, but it was moving kind of fast. We seemed to be the only African American people in the whole auditorium. When we got to the registration table, Jamal announced, "My name is Jamal Washington, and I am here to exercise my right to become a first-class jelly bean counter."

I couldn't help but laugh. "Ma Ma, that's what Ma Dear used to say when she went to register to vote."

"Let me see here," the man behind the table said. "Washington, Washington . . . here it is—Washington. What's your first name again, son?"

"Jamal."

"I have some Washingtons here, but I don't see Jamal. I guess you never registered."

"Never registered?" I asked. "I was the one who registered him. Jamal, give me your iPad." I powered it up and went to my email. "See? There it is. It says Confirmed!"

"I'm sorry, boys. We just don't have any record of it. You'll have to try again next year," he told Jamal. "Now move along. Others are waiting in line."

I remembered learning back in Freedom School that you could be taken off the voter registration list if you had a "Negro-sounding" name and I wondered. I raised my arms, clenched my fists, waved them in the air, and yelled, *"This* is what suppression looks like for kids! And 'we ain't gonna let no-body turn us around!'"

I looked at Jamal and saw the disappointment in his eyes turn to determination. We fist bumped and high fived. Then Jamal looked back at the man at the table and said loudly, "Yes, I *will* be back next year!"

Jamal and Me: Freedom Summer

* * * * * * *

FREEDOM SUMMER did help spark reform, partly due to how it educated the country about voter suppression. In 1964, Congress passed the Civil Rights Act, followed by the Voting Rights Act in 1965. But in a way, Blacks were better off a century earlier.

In 1865, after the Civil War ended, four million Black Americans were freed. During a period called Reconstruction from 1865 to 1877, federal troops were sent to Southern states to protect the rights of these people. More than half a million Southern Black men became voters. (Women of any color still couldn't vote.) About two thousand Black men were elected to offices and made changes to support African Americans. Hiram Rhodes Revels became the first African American senator. He represented Mississippi in Congress from 1870 to 1871.[2]

Sadly, the positive changes didn't last long. When the federal troops were withdrawn from the South in 1877, White supremacists took control again, suppressing Black Americans' civil and voting rights. At the time of Freedom Summer in 1964, the situation for Blacks in Mississippi remained dismal. The state had no African American state representatives.

Today, in 2022, Mississippi African Americans are still suppressed in many ways. However, the state has one African American representative in Congress—Bennie Thompson, from the Mississippi Delta.

* * * * * * *

About the Author

Author and native of south Minneapolis, Minnesota, **J. Darnell Johnson** loves to tell stories from the African American experience that put culture at the center. His style is both creative and fun. He helps the reader, both children and adults, vividly engage with the characters, their emotions, and their story.

J. Darnell has a Master's degree in Organizational Management from Concordia University in St. Paul, Minnesota. He is a Bush Leadership Fellow and has traveled to Ghana, West Africa, to learn about the culture.

He has over thirty years of experience working in social services, primarily in the fields of Child Protection, Juvenile Justice, and Runaway and Homeless. Ten of those years, he worked in African American culture-specific programs as an emergency shelter and group home program director. Whether he's portraying Malcolm X on his birthday, performing a Black history rap, teaching Kwanzaa to elementary school students, or engaging in other supportive endeavors, J. Darnell has spent a life-long career serving his community.

Currently, J. Darnell Johnson lives with his wife in Burnsville, Minnesota. As Workforce Development Supervisor at Goodwill-Easterseals he empowers Dad's to connect/reconnect with their children.

He enjoys listening and dancing to "old school" rhythm and blues music, taking walks by the lake, and watching his favorite football team, the Minnesota Vikings.

About the Author

J. Darnell's first children's book, *Roots Four Zero*, shares a journey to freedom. A fourteen-year-old slave girl named Zero and her newfound companions run away to find their roots and their essence. (Amazon.com)

The Opening is science fiction/fantasy with an ending rivaling that of the original *Planet of the Apes* movie. A black "hue-man" being from the planet Kebb thinks the grass must be greener on the other side of the galaxy. He and his family travel through a stargate called The Opening, only to find themselves on planet Earth during the time of slavery. (Amazon.com)

Jamal and Me is a story in which, due to no fault of their own, Jamal and Jordan are taken away by police to an emergency shelter. There, with an unrelenting desire to return home, they must rely on each other. (strivepublishing.com/store)

Just Due is a Science Fiction/Fantasy story. In the year 3033, a crooked power couple gets taken for a ride of a lifetime! (blacksciencefictionsociety.com) In *Genesis* magazine.

In *One to the Other,* Jack and his girlfriend Pearl experience mysterious happenings, and only Jack knows their secret. (blacksciencefictionsociety.com) In *Genesis* magazine.

Sit Com takes you on a trip through America's ugly racial past and foretells its uncertain future. (blacksciencefictionsociety.com) In *Genesis Anthology of Science Fiction*, Book II.

"They Have No Business Knowing Any of This" is a poem that marvels at the science of the Dogon people of West Africa, who have no access to scientific instruments. (talkingriverreview.com)

Soon to be published is *Ol' Jim Crow's Jubilee Day Caper.* In the year 1890, Ol' Jim Crow, who lives on a cloud, is determined to stop African Americans from celebrating Juneteenth.

In 2021, J. Darnell Johnson won the Writing for Social Change Award bestowed by Planting People Growing Justice

Author's Note on Truth vs. Fiction

Jamal and Me: Freedom Summer is historical fiction. That means I added made-up, or fictional, characters to real historical people and events. Historical fiction can also include fantasy elements. I would like to help you separate the truth from the fiction.

First the fiction:

Jamal, Jordan, Pharaoh, Ma Ma, Grandma Lynn, Ma Dear, Grandpa Shack, and Moc are all fictional characters. They did not actually live in history. The fourth Sunday, known in the story as the Big Day, did not happen in Ruleville, Mississippi, as far as my research could take me. However, my family celebrated it and made it officially our family reunion in Marshall, Texas. It was most popular during the 1960s to the 1980s.

Jamal called the Big Day "Freedom Sunday." This wasn't a real event in Ruleville, Mississippi. Some churches across the country use the term Freedom Sunday for Sundays when people have the freedom to talk about political candidates openly to deepen their understanding of God's love for justice. Or Freedom Sunday might be a time for a call to action for a just cause. The term is not necessarily used by Black churches or advocates for civil rights.

Next the fantasy:

Queen Azina and the Azziza people are all fantasy characters, and traveling back in time is also fantasy. Both fiction and fantasy are imaginary, but fiction is something that *could* have existed. Fantasy is something that *could not* have existed or happened—at least that we know of at this point in time.

And the historical truth:

Fannie Lou Hamer, Pap Hamer, Vergie and Dorothy Jean Hamer, and Bob Moses were real people.

Author's Note on Truth vs. Fiction

The murders of James Chaney, Andrew Goodman, and Mickey Schwerner and the funeral of James Chaney in Meridian, Mississippi, really happened.

Freedom fighters existed, as did civil rights activists Dave Dennis, Harry Belafonte, John Lewis, Julian Bond, and James Forman.

Freedom Summer and the Mississippi Summer Project are historical.

"Literacy" tests in which people were asked to guess the number of jelly beans in a jar and the number of bubbles in a bar of soap were all true circumstances that happened from the 1850s to the 1960s. Of course, guessing the number of jelly beans in a jar is possible because there's a fixed number in the jar. But trying to guess the number of bubbles in a bar of soap was impossible—and even the clerk wouldn't know and could say you were wrong no matter what you said.

In the story of Jamal and Me, Jamal was able to count the number of jelly beans and correctly guess the number of bubbles in a bar of soap. However, if you were African American, it was extremely rare that the registration clerk said you passed the test. He or she would simply say you failed. This naturally led African Americans to give up, and they would never return.

Medgar Evers, the man Fannie Lou Hamer mentioned had died, was a Black Mississippi civil rights hero. He was shot and killed by a White supremacist.

The acts of voter suppression in the story were not unlike other acts of voter suppression throughout the South during the early 1960s. They could have happened to almost anyone who was African American during that time and place.

African Americans were living in a caste system, even though America was said to be a democracy. A caste system divides people into different levels of society depending on the family people are born into, so they can't escape it. The system was designed to keep the privileges of Whites and keep the Blacks with almost none, if any.

Real-Life Freedom Summer Characters

Fannie Lou Townsend Hamer was born into humble circumstances in the Mississippi Delta. She became one of the most important, passionate, and powerful voices of the civil and voting rights movements. In addition, she led efforts to create greater economic opportunities for African Americans.

Fannie Lou Hamer helped organize Freedom Summer in 1964. This project brought hundreds of college students, both Black and White, to help with African American voter registration in the segrega-ted South. Also in 1964, she announced she was running for the Mississippi House of Representatives, but she was barred from the ballot. A year later, Hamer, Victoria Gray, and Annie Devine became the first Black women to stand in the U.S. Congress when they unsuccessfully protested the Mississippi House election of 1964. She traveled a great deal, giving powerful speeches on behalf of civil rights. In 1971, Hamer helped to found the National Women's Political Caucus.

Frustrated by the political process, Hamer turned to economics as a strategy for greater racial equality. In 1968, she began a "pig bank" to provide free pigs for Black farmers to breed, raise, and slaughter. A year later, she launched the Freedom Farm Cooperative (FFC), buying up land that Blacks could own and farm together. With the assistance of donors (including famed singer Harry Belafonte), she purchased 640 acres and launched a coop store, boutique, and sewing enterprise. She had 200 units of low-income housing built, and many still exist in Ruleville. The FFC lasted until the mid-1970s. In its best days, it was among the largest employers in Sunflower County. Extensive travel and fundraising took Hamer away from the day-to-day operations, as did her failing health, and the FFC eventually folded. In 1977, Fannie Lou Hamer died of breast cancer at age fifty-nine. (Photograph[3])

Robert Parris (Bob) Moses was a soft-spoken civil rights organizer from Harlem, New York City, who helped Blacks in some of the most dangerous parts of the South, including the Mississippi Delta. Moses worked with the Council of Federated Organizations (COFO), which combined the Mississippi branches of the four major civil rights organizations. As part of this work, Moses was the main organi-zer of the Freedom Summer Project in 1964, which recruited hundreds of student volunteers. He was also deeply involved in the Mississippi Freedom Democratic Party, which he co-founded with Fannie Lou Hamer. This party challenged the all-white Mississippi delegation to the 1964 Democratic National Convention. Moses wanted to empower and learn from the people he worked with and helped.

He later ran the Algebra Project, an effort to increase math training in poor communities and prepare students for the workforce.

Real-Life Freedom Summer Characters

Bob Moses died in July of 2021. (Photograph[4])

Author's Note on Voter Suppression

I wrote this book for young people to learn about voter suppression and hopefully help resolve and eliminate it over time. Suppression has reared its ugly head over and over throughout the history of the United States, particularly in the South. Black people have not been the only target of suppression. At one time, only White men who owned property could legally vote.

Voter suppression comes in many, many forms. Basically, certain groups of people want to keep particular people in power, while keeping others out of power. To do this, they find ways to keep their opponents from voting and making their voices heard. They make them jump through hoops and wear them down with requirements.

Voter suppression can sometimes seem like it's fair and harmless. Thus, some people might go a long time without questioning it and exercising their rights. Those who support voter suppression usually defend it by saying they're trying to stop voter fraud. In the case of fraud, some votes are faked to help a certain group, and thus the results of an election are false. However, there's never been any evidence of widespread voter fraud in U.S. elections—ever.

In the case of voter suppression, some people are kept or discouraged from voting, so the election results don't reflect the views of all eligible voters. Voter suppression can weaken our democracy and violate our rights as citizens.

What Suppression Might Look Like for a Black Child

The situation in Mississippi was called voter suppression. The Whites didn't out-and-out tell the Blacks they couldn't vote, but they figured out sneaky ways to stop them.

Following are three examples of what suppression might look like for a Black child, although the outcome isn't as serious as voter suppression:

Each week you put part of your allowance in an old coffee can to save for a new bicycle. When you have enough money to buy it, the store clerk says the price has gone up. So, you return a month later with more money. The clerk shakes his head and says the price has gone up again. You do this repeatedly. The next time you go to the store, you notice a White boy's parents are buying him the same bike for the price it was in the beginning.

You go to your local kids' club and fill out a membership application so you can be part of the Peer Counseling team. The clerk says, "Thank you, and you will be notified by mail in three days that your application was accepted."

You don't receive anything in a week, so you return to the club and ask about your application. The clerk tells you that it was thrown away because it was incorrectly filled out and you'll have to complete another one.

You complete the application and the same thing happens.

Jamal and Me: Freedom Summer

It's thrown out for incorrect information, even though you checked it over and over.

It happens for a third time. You check with your school teacher, and he says it was written correctly. You get so frustrated you give up on being a peer counselor.

———————————

You enter into a sweepstakes drawing at your local sports club for a brand new bicycle. The rules are you can only enter once and your name has to match the same name you wrote on your membership application.

When the winner is announced, it isn't you. You go to the clerk and ask if your name was entered in the drawing. She tells you that your name was thrown out because it didn't match the name on the application. It said Thurmond Hall on the application, but when you entered your name in the drawing, you wrote Thurmond Hall, Jr.

———————————

If you find yourself in a situation where you're being unfairly treated because of your race, report it to an adult you trust. Here are organizations that may be able to help:

- Kids in Need of Defense (KIND)
  https://supportkind.org/who-we-are/contact-us/
  1-202-824-8680
- Black Lives Matter (BLM)
  https://blacklivesmatter.com/contact/
- The Black Youth Project
  http://blackyouthproject.com/contact/

What Suppression Might Look Like for a Black Child

- American Civil Liberties Union (ACLU)
  https://www.aclu.org/about/affiliates?redirect=affiliates
  1-212-549-2500
- National Association for the Advancement of Colored People (NAACP)
  https://naacp.org/contact

Teachers' Resources

Teachers may want to explain to children some or all of the following information as examples.

Here are just a few recent acts of voter suppression leading up to the 2020 elections:

- Two people were charged with making false robocalls to residents in largely Black Detroit. The call said if they voted by mail, they could face debt collection and forced vaccination. – *USA Today,* October 1, 2020

- Some Black voters in Detroit received a mailing that falsely claimed they had until November 10th to vote due to COVID-19 concerns, when the final date to vote was November 3rd. – *USA Today,* October 29, 2020

- Both California and Boston have had ballot boxes set on fire, destroying dozens of ballots. – *USA Today,* October 26, 2020

- Seven states have strict photo identification laws. Voters must present one of certain forms of government-issued photo ID to cast a regular ballot. No exceptions. These strict ID laws are part of an ongoing strategy to suppress the vote, and it works. The U.S. Government Accountability Office estimates Voter ID laws reduce voter turnout by two to three percentage points, translating to tens of thousands of votes lost in a single state. – *ACLU.org,* May 28, 2020

- A Tennessee poll worker was fired for asking voters to turn their shirts supporting Black Lives Matter inside out,

Teachers' Resources

violating his training as a nonpartisan election worker, according to a local election commission. – CNN, October 20, 2020

Today many states are practicing voter suppression through the following tactics. These unfair actions often target Black and minority voters:

- gerrymandering (change of voting district boundaries to advantage certain groups)
- voter roll purges
- voter ID laws
- voter precinct closures
- elimination of Sunday voting and early voting
- criminalization of voter registration drives

These five organizations fight against voter suppression:

1. **American Civil Liberties Union (ALCU)**
   https://www.aclu.org/
2. **Fair Fight**
   https://fairfight.com/
3. **National Democratic Redistricting Committee**
   https://democraticredistricting.com/
4. **Protect Democracy**
   https://protectdemocracy.org/
5. **Let America Vote**
   https://letamericavote.org/

This information may be useful for people who are old enough to vote when exercising their right to vote. Children can share these suggestions with their parents or older siblings.

- The Voter Protection Hotline is run by lawyers. They're helpful if you have questions on anything from finding your polling place to registering to vote. They can also help you on election day while you're at the polls. Call: 1-866-Our-Vote (1-866-687-8683)

- Always check your local city hall office to see if you're registered to vote. If you're registered, make sure your information is correct and up to date.

- Plan how you're going to get to your polling place and what time you want to get there.

- Get informed. Find out from your local city hall what documents you will need to vote.

- If you're not old enough to vote, ask your parents if you can go with them inside the voting booth and watch how the voting process works.

- When you arrive at your polling place, if they can't find your name on the voter rolls, ask for a provisional ballot.

- Once you do vote, take a photo of your ballot in case you need evidence later.

- If you make a mistake on your ballot, ask for a new one.

- If voting machines are not working at your polling place, ask for a paper ballot.

- If you're not old enough to vote, you can still help others. You can remind voters of all of the above. You can also ask voters to volunteer at a polling place.

Teachers' Resources

- Remember, if you run into any problems on voting day, don't hesitate to call 1-866-Our-Vote (1-866-687-8683)!

Websites for voting and civics education for kids:

Kids Voting USA
https://kidsvotingusa.org/

iCivics
https://www.icivics.org/

Constitution Center
https://constitutioncenter.org/learn/educational-resources/we-the-civics-kids/

Center for Civic Education
https://www.civiced.org/voting-lessons/

Civics Education Resource Guide
https://www.ncsc.org/education-and-careers/civics-education/resource-guide

Edutopia
https://www.edutopia.org/article/civics-elementary-classroom

Glossary of Terms

Caste system: Also known as Jim Crow. The caste system divides people into different levels or classes of society depending on the family people are born into, so they can't escape it. The system was designed to keep the privileges of Whites and keep the Blacks with almost none, if any. It maintained racial inequality in the South.

Civil rights workers: People who work on behalf of the country's citizens to protect the rights given to them by the nation's government.

COFO: Council of Federated Organizations, a combination of major civil rights organizations operating in Mississippi to coordinate and support voter registration and other civil rights activities.

CORE: Congress for Racial Equality. Its mission is to bring about equality for all people regardless of race, creed, sex, age, disability, sexual orientation, religion, or ethnic background.

Colored people: A term that was used earlier in our country's history for Black or African American people. Today it is considered offensive to African Americans.

Commie: Short for communist. An unfriendly term that White southerners called people from the north who opposed their way of life.

Constitution: The set of basic laws by which a nation, state, or other organization is governed.

Glossary of Terms

Democracy: A form of government in which power rests with the people, either directly or through elected representatives.

Dixiecrat: Those people of the southern Democratic political party who opposed civil rights programs.

Election ballot: A sheet of paper on which people who are voting indicate their choices.

Endorsement: A statement given in support of a person or product, as in a political campaign or an advertisement.

Gerrymandering: Changing the boundaries of election districts to favor a particular political party.

Good moral character clause: Mississippi added a requirement in 1960 that people must have "good moral character" to vote as part of a series of attempts to stifle Black voter registration. The Voting Rights Act, passed in 1965, got rid of moral character voting requirements.

FBI: Federal Bureau of Investigation. The U.S. government agency responsible for investigating crimes against national laws.

First-class citizen: A member of a class of individuals who receive fair treatment by its nation with all of its protections.

Freedom Riders: A group of civil rights activists that participated in freedom rides throughout the South to protest unfair practices toward African Americans in public facilities and other unjust acts.

Freedom Schools: Schools in 1960s Mississippi that educated students in social justice.

Freedom Summer: Also known as Mississippi Summer Project or Freedom Summer Project. The purpose was to register African American voters, educate African Americans in social justice, and develop the Mississippi Democratic Freedom Party throughout the state of Mississippi.

Harambee: An African Swahili word that means "All pull together."

Integrated: To bring together and make open to all cultures and races.

Juke joint: A small roadside business where you can eat, drink, dance, and listen to music played from a jukebox.

KKK or Ku Klux Klan or just the Klan: A group of white supremacists, or people who think the white race is better than other races. KKK groups have been active on and off in American history. In the South in the 1960s, Klan members opposed the civil rights movement and its leaders. They sought to terrorize any African Americans who tried to vote.

Literacy tests: Questions asked of people who wanted to register to vote that they had to answer correctly to pass and be able to vote. The tests were designed to keep African Americans and poor Whites from voting by asking them questions that were almost impossible or impossible to answer correctly. The tests for Whites

Glossary of Terms

asked easy questions to answer in order to vote. The Voting Rights Act, passed in 1965, got rid of literacy test requirements.

Mississippi Delta: A region in northwest Mississippi that had the highest rate of poor people and one of the highest numbers of African Americans of any state in the 1960s.

MDFP: Mississippi Democratic Freedom Party, formed in Mississippi by Blacks and Whites to challenge the Mississippi Democratic Party, which during the early 1960s allowed only White participation.

NAACP: National Association for the Advancement of Colored People, an organization that works for equal rights for African Americans.

Negro people: A term formerly used for Black or African American people. Today it is considered offensive to African Americans.

Plantation: A large farm or estate for growing rubber, cotton, or other crops to sell.

Preamble to the Constitution: A brief introductory statement describing the purposes and principles of the Constitution.

Polling place: A place where you go to vote in an election.

Poll tax: A tax you had to pay before you could vote. The Voting Rights Act passed in 1965 got rid of poll tax requirements.

Jamal and Me: Freedom Summer

Provisional ballot: A ballot used to record a vote when there's a question about a given voter's eligibility that must be resolved before the vote can count.

SCLC: Southern Christian Leadership Conference, a civil rights organization fighting for the civil rights of African Americans. Rev. Dr. Martin Luther King, Jr. was its first president.

Sharecropper: A farmer paying rent to live on a landowner's land by harvesting crops for the landowner.

SNCC: Student Nonviolent Coordinating Committee, a student-led civil rights organization that played a central role in the Civil Rights Movement.

Swahili: A native language spoken by people who live mostly in East Africa.

Taxation without representation is tyranny: A political slogan meaning that, if you're being taxed, you should have people representing your interests in political office. Tyranny means a government in which a single person rules absolutely and in a cruel way.

Unlawful assembly: An illegal meeting of three or more people likely to cause a breach of the peace or endanger the public. This term of law was often falsely used in Mississippi and other parts of the South during 1950s and 1960s to stop protest marches for civil rights.

Glossary of Terms

Voter fraud: Illegal behavior of individual voters, such as voting more than once or voting as another person, or violating other voting rules.

Voter intimidation: A person's attempt to scare you into not voting with threatening behavior.

Voter purge: Deleting names from a registered voter list for various reasons, one of which may be to keep certain voters from voting.

Voter registration: Signing up to vote, which is a requirement for qualified voters to vote.

Voter roll: A list of persons who are qualified to vote.

White Citizens Council: A council of mostly White men whose aim was to intimidate, or scare, African Americans and oppose their rights to keep them from gaining any personal power.

Voter suppression: Strategies used to influence the outcome of an election by discouraging or preventing specific groups of people from voting.

White supremacist: A person who believes that Whites are superior to any other race just by being born White.

Yank: Short for Yankee. An unfriendly term that White southerners called people from the north who opposed their way of life.

Endnotes

[1] Bonnie Worth, *One Vote, Two Votes, I Vote, You Vote.* Penguin Random House, Cat in the Hat's Learning Library, 2016, p. 8.

[2] Artika R. Tyner, *Black Voter Suppression: The Fight for the Right to Vote.* Minneapolis: Lerner Publications, 2021.

[3] Photograph of Fannie Lou Hamer at the Democratic National Convention, Atlantic City, New Jersey, August 1964. Wikimedia Commons, courtesy of *U.S. World & News Report* Collection at the Library of Congress.

[4] Photograph of Bob Moses in Princeton, New Jersey, John Witherspoon Middle School Auditorium. Flickr, courtesy of Princeton Public Library.